LISBON WATER KILLS

Axel G. Barry

Mark,

Hope you enjoy and learn more about Portugal from this.

Axel G.

Copyright © Axel Bugge and Barry Hatton 2014

The moral rights of the authors have been asserted.

All characters in this novel are fictitious and any resemblance to real persons, living or dead, is purely coincidental.

All rights reserved. This book or any portion of it may not be reproduced in any manner without the express permission of the authors, except for brief quotations in reviews.

Contact: https://www.facebook.com/pages/Lisbon-Water-Kills/728835457137176?fref=nf

For our families

Thanks to

Peter Fay
Frederico de Melo Franco and
Lina Maria Rincon

Chapter 1

It was as if the two bodies raced the raindrops to the ground, falling fast, faster, unimpeded. The torrential rain muffled the thud when the women hit the street, within seconds of each other. Like the raindrops, nothing else stopped them falling. There was no screaming, just immediate death as they dropped from the tower 45 meters above and crumpled into lumps on the pretty black and white patterns of the Portuguese pavement. The noisy, pouring rain swiftly washed away the blood, for a few moments turning the rivulets red as they streamed into the gutter. It was quick and clean.

Nobody noticed the bodies for a while. The relentless rain had driven the Lisbon tourists away as the late autumn evening darkened the riverside downtown district. Shopkeepers had closed their businesses and gone home through the lashing storm. Only occasional buses and taxis braved the roads, following the water's path of least resistance down the main roads into the old part of the city that is Lisbon's lowest point, by the Tagus River. The runoff flowed quickly, forming rising streams and puddles and forcing Francisco to drive his taxi in the middle of the road to avoid the rising water by the sidewalk. He spotted the bodies just as he was wondering how Lisbon could cope with the deluge that night – in twenty years on the job he had never seen so much water in the streets.

Above, the grey iron girders of the Elevador de Santa Justa were shiny with wetness. The two dead women were lying at the foot of the steps that led up to the century-old street elevator, a landmark which stands like a tall straight little piece of the Eiffel Tower. In summer, tourists queued here to take the wood-paneled lift from the street called Rua do Ouro up to the Carmo Square, sparing further effort by thighs fit to burst after hours on old Lisbon's hilly streets. At first glance, Francisco thought the bodies were two tramps, perhaps sleeping off their cheap red wine. But no, that couldn't be right. Something was wrong – the clothes, or the hair, he couldn't put his finger on it. Nobody could sleep through this downpour.

He slowed to a stop and peered through the passenger window, trying to make out details through the thick rain and murky light. He didn't want to get out of his cab in this weather. But he couldn't just drive away. He cursed, and put his hazard warning lights on, jumping out in the middle of the street while nothing was coming. His shoes made a splash as he got out. He held a newspaper over his head and sprang across the few paces separating him from the bodies. He leaned over them. The pounding rain was confusing. It made it hard for him to see and think. He prodded one of the bodies in its sodden clothes. He saw it was a young woman with red hair and a tattoo on her neck. He shook the other body slightly, his sense of panic rising quickly. It, too, was a young woman. Then he noticed the bloody mess of the smashed skull.

*

Antonia Fortunata watched patiently as the waiter poured a splash of red wine into her glass and took a step back for her to taste it. It was quiet in the restaurant, with just a few other customers dotted around the discreet corners of the room. The filthy weather in Lisbon was keeping the usual dinner custom away.

Antonia held the glass up to the light to observe the wine's color, swirled it around, sniffed it, and took a delicate sip. Miguel couldn't help letting out a snigger.

"You been taking a course?" he asked.

"Maybe," Antonia said, with a sly smile. "I've been doing a lot these last few years you don't know about."

"Well it's a good thing we're catching up then," Miguel said.

The waiter leaned forward, nudging Antonia to make a decision.

"That's nice stuff," Antonia told him, and the waiter filled both glasses.

"'Nice stuff'?" Miguel said as the waiter walked away. "I don't think that's a very sophisticated term for wine."

"It was a cheap course," Antonia said.

"Unlike the wine," Miguel said.

"It's nice here," Antonia said, looking around. "I could never afford this kind of thing in the States. Not on a cop's pay."

They both drank. They could hear the rain beating outside, louder than the murmur of the other diners.

"Some things never change," Miguel said. "Of course you insisted on trying the wine yourself, even though he offered it to the man at the table – i.e., me. I always suspected you had a stray Y chromosome in you somewhere, despite your womanly good looks."

Antonia smiled. "I'm not going to rise to the bait. That's what I would have done before. But I've still got my own mind, thank you very much."

"Let's drink to that," Miguel said, raising his glass. "A toast."

Antonia pushed her long, brown curly hair from one side of her face. "All right," she said, picking up her glass. "What shall we drink to?"

Miguel looked thoughtful. "How about, *A la recherche du temps perdu*?"

"Oh-oh. I forgot you went to college, Mr. Smart-ass Detective."

Miguel smiled. "Sorry. It means, In Search of Lost Time. It's a famous book."

"Well, all right then. I did actually know that. But I don't like to dwell on the past," Antonia said, stiffening a little. "I prefer to look forward."

"Very well. In search of our future time, then," Miguel said, and Antonia raised one eyebrow.

They drank, both wondering whether they had a future together and, if so, what kind of future.

They looked over the menu. Antonia fancied the cod fried in olive oil, but she was watching her figure. She had a weakness for Portuguese food and she'd put on weight over the last few months since she had moved back to Lisbon.

Once they had ordered, Miguel sat back and picked up his glass. "You're fully recovered from the shooting, I suppose. I mean, you haven't mentioned any problems," he said, trying not to pry too much, which he remembered she hated. But he at least wanted to show he was concerned.

"My problems are my problems," Antonia said.

"Right," Miguel said, putting his glass down. "You really haven't changed much."

Antonia allowed herself a smile. Miguel admired her full red lips and shoulder-length brown hair and couldn't stop himself thinking about the passionate romance they once had.

"We're older now," Antonia said. "And wiser. So we won't get in too deep, like last time."

Miguel scratched his suntanned shaved head, then stroked his jaw. He had kept his muscular build and strong face into middle age, Antonia thought to herself.

"I presume you know about my problems," he said. "Someone in the family must have spilled the beans. Gossip gets around like wildfire in this village called Portugal."

"Yeah, sorry. I heard," Antonia said. Miguel's marital problems had, in fact, been the talk of her Portuguese family for many months, and everyone was expecting him and his wife to separate at any moment.

"You know what it's like, a cop's life," Miguel said. "My wife's lonely and jealous of every woman I work with. My son – he's eight now – is resentful because I'm never at home. I don't blame them. I always seem to be working. I'm lonely too, but what can I do? It's getting worse, with the spending cuts and staff cuts and everything. I have to do the work of three men. For less money, with the new taxes." He took a gulp of wine. "Truth is, I'm as lonely as they are," he said, and gave Antonia a meaningful look.

"Whoa, cowboy, slow down," Antonia said.

"No, no, I'm not going to make a pass at you or anything like that. I mean, it's just good to see you again, like this."

"Sure," Antonia said, not wanting to be hard on him and unsure of her own feelings after all that had happened. She had never got married, though she'd booked her trip to the altar with a local sheriff before it became crystal clear that marrying him would have been a big mistake. And here she was now, in her early forties, uncertain whether to be sad or glad.

Miguel's cellphone rang. He pulled it out of his pocket and peered at the number. "I'll have to take this, it's work," he said.

"No sweat. I still remember what it's like being a cop."

Miguel listened on the phone, rolled his eyes to Antonia, then said "OKAY" and hung up.

"I'm sorry, I need to go," he said.

"Something big?"

"Two dead women downtown. Foreigners, it looks like."

"Sounds like a job for the Caped Crusader," Antonia said. She took her napkin off her lap and threw it on the table. "Which means, I'm coming with you," she said, standing up.

"I know you well enough not to try and stop you," Miguel said, following her to the door. "Just remember who's in charge." But Antonia was already out of earshot.

*

Miguel turned his windscreen wipers onto the fastest speed. There wasn't much traffic but he couldn't drive fast because the streets of the downtown district, known as the Baixa, were being deluged by the lashing rain.

"Oh my God," he said. "I don't think I've ever seen it this bad."

"The drains must be blocked," Antonia said. "The streets are filling up."

"That's always been a problem down here near the river," Miguel said, peering through the sheets of rain. "There are loads of streams running under the buildings. Dumb to build on top of them, if you ask me. If there's a high tide in the Tagus River it makes it worse. The water's got nowhere to go."

They got to the Rua do Ouro and saw the police lights flashing around the foot of the Elevador de Santa Justa. Buttoning up their coats, Miguel and Antonia stepped out of the car and into water that lapped at the top of their shoes. Antonia followed Miguel to where the emergency crews were bunched on the pavement around a bright spotlight from a police car.

"Hey," Miguel said, raising his voice to be heard through the noisy rain. "Miguel Soares." He flashed his badge. "What have we got?"

"Two women," one of the policemen said. "Looks from their ID cards like they're Germans. We haven't found their passports."

Miguel crouched over the bodies, blinking against the rain, and said, "Get some kind of cover in here. A tarpaulin or something. It's impossible to work like this."

One of the emergency crew held an umbrella over Miguel. They noticed Antonia, like men usually did, but assumed she was some official accompanying the detective. She stayed just behind him and kept quiet.

Miguel pushed aside the raincoat that had been placed over one of the mangled bodies. The woman was wearing loose clothes in bright colors. She wore beads and bangles and her long hair was dyed blue. He shuffled across to the other body. Same kind of clothes but a cropped, punk hair style and heavy boots. Their skulls were split open and their limbs stuck out at crazy angles.

Antonia, craning her neck over Miguel's back, suddenly looked alarmed. She covered her mouth with her hand and quickly turned away. The others thought she was queasy at the sight of blood.

"Looks like they're about 30," Miguel said to nobody in particular.

"That's right," the policeman said. "Their IDs say 28 and 29."

"Anybody see anything?" Miguel asked.

"Nope. A taxi driver came across them, called it in," the policeman said.

"Right then, go and start knocking on doors," Miguel said. "I know all the shops are closed, but maybe someone saw something. I mean, this is not an everyday occurrence down here," he said, standing up and lifting one foot out of the rising water. "And what the hell is it with all this goddamn water everywhere, what's going on?"

"Must be blocked drains," one of the crew said.

"Jesus Christ. Somebody had better warn the city council," Miguel said, looking around for Antonia. "Once forensics are done let's get the bodies off for the autopsy. They're pretty smashed up. Maybe it was a hit-and-run."

"Maybe they fell off there," one of the policemen said, pointing up into the rain.

Everyone looked up at the iron girders of the Elevador de Santa Justa and the observation deck on top of it.

"That'd certainly kill you," Miguel said. "But fall over that railing? I don't think so. Unless it was suicide. Or something."

"Senhor Soares?"

Miguel turned around.

"How do you do? My name is Wolfgang Müller. I am the police liaison officer at the German embassy," he said, showing Miguel his ID and extending his hand beneath his umbrella. "You will inform me please about what you are doing regarding the case of these two unfortunate German ladies."

Miguel looked Wolfgang up and down. He was in his mid-50s and wore an impeccably tailored charcoal-gray suit beneath a long raincoat. The sophisticated look was, however, tempered by his green wellington boots. "Well, you're certainly dressed for the occasion," Miguel said. "My superiors will keep the embassy informed, I'm sure."

"You will excuse me," Wolfgang said. "I think you will find we are supposed to work, how do you say, in combination. I would like to help you. I can get you information from the German side. Forgive me if sometimes I come across as brusque. I am not speaking my native language. Please be patient." He gave Miguel a friendly smile.

"Well, okay, we'll see what the autopsy gives us. You certainly got here promptly. German efficiency, I suppose. I'll be in touch," Miguel said. He spotted Antonia standing in the cover of a shop doorway across the road and went over.

"You all right?"

"Yeah, I suppose," Antonia said, lighting a cigarette. "I knew them."

"You knew them! Where from?"

"Back in the summer when I was travelling around, trying to get my head together. They lived in a kind of hippie commune down south, in Aljezur, you know, that charming little village on the coast. It's Brigitte and Katja. I liked them. We weren't best friends or anything but they were nice to me when I needed it."

"I'm sorry," Miguel said. "You'll have to tell me everything you know about them." He put his hand gently on Antonia's arm, though he knew she could keep her composure.

"Who's the guy in the Armani suit and wellington boots?" Antonia asked, dragging on her cigarette.

Miguel glanced back over his shoulder. Wolfgang was watching them through the rain. "He's from the German embassy. He seems all right. He's offered to help."

Antonia took a drag on her cigarette and looked at the rainwater sloshing down the street. "The bodies are going to get swept away at this rate," she said. "It's like a monsoon."

"Yeah, it doesn't look good," Miguel said.

Gathering forensic evidence at the scene became impossible with the rising water, which was now ankle-deep. The policemen began to get cold and nervous, knowing they had no equipment to properly secure the crime scene. One policeman tried to cover the bodies by clumsily holding two umbrellas over them.

"This really is a joke," Antonia said as she watched with Miguel from across the street. "Do you guys have any proper equipment at all?"

"Haven't you heard about our austerity measures? Portugal was almost bankrupt before it got its bailout, you know. We've hardly got enough money for petrol and bullets. You think there's any money for new equipment?" Miguel said, glancing up and down the street. "We've got to get these bodies out of here."

Miguel splashed his way across the road, soaking wet now and not bothering any more to shield himself from the rain, and ordered one of his staff to get an ambulance. But the crime scene was quickly becoming a secondary concern for the emergency services as the floodwaters rose alarmingly. The deluge forced the policemen to grab hold of the bodies to stop them being washed away. Then they heard loud crashing sounds a few blocks away, down towards the river.

Antonia, trying to prevent the water coming over the top of her ankle-length boots, went over to Miguel. "What the hell was that?" she asked apprehensively.

The policemen who knew Lisbon better could only imagine the worst: the ancient tunnels under many buildings in the area had probably started to cave in under the weight of the water.

"I dread to think it could be the tunnels. But it certainly sounds like buildings collapsing," Miguel said.

Sirens began to scream around them. A convoy of fire engines pushed their way down the street, plowing through the water and sending out waves that made it even harder for the police to keep hold of the two bodies. Army jeeps and trucks from a nearby barracks followed close behind. Helicopters hovered overhead, their spotlights peering through the sheets of driving rain that battered the downtown district.

"This is an evacuation. Please move to higher ground," shouted a voice through a loudspeaker attached to one of the helicopters. "Emergency services are on their way. Please remain calm."

The policemen were trained to deal with stressful situations but none of them had ever been through anything like this. It felt like Lisbon was under siege.

"This is completely surreal," said Miguel, squinting against the rain as he glanced up at the night sky.

The call to evacuate worked. Soon, people appeared along the deserted Rua do Ouro, splashing through the water in the dark and looking suspiciously at the policemen bent over the two lifeless forms. A few civil servants who worked late in the downtown government buildings walked by, holding briefcases over their heads as they struggled up the street. But it was mostly frail, old people who passed by – the ones who had lived all their lives in this part of town due to century-old rent controls that kept their homes cheap but discouraged landlords from modernizing their buildings.

Miguel thought about relieving his men to help with the evacuation, but his main responsibility was still the two bodies which were almost floating. The ambulance had still not arrived.

"You've got to do something, quickly," Antonia told Miguel quietly, not wanting to draw the attention of the other policemen.

One of the policemen was on his radio to the ambulance service.

"They can't get down here. They say the closest place where it's dry enough is up at the square," the policeman said.

"Okay, you two," Miguel shouted, pointing to two policemen. "There must be stretchers in those fire engines. Go and get them and we'll take the bodies out ourselves."

Antonia looked at Wolfgang, who had stayed close to them the whole time despite the rain and the chaos. She felt like he was staring at her.

"Don't you have to get back and do a report or something?" she asked him.

"No, I am free in my work. I choose the best method," he said.

The policemen returned with the stretchers and Miguel directed them to carefully pick up the twisted bodies. It was hard – the men were not used to handling mangled bodies like these, especially as they were drenched and the rain and floodwaters gave them no respite. Worried that they might pull the bodies apart, they eased them gingerly onto the stretchers.

Four men picked up each stretcher, and the group joined others walking out of the Baixa. It was tough going at first, but the water level ebbed as they moved towards the square and higher ground.

Dom Pedro IV Square had become the center of the evacuation operation. Ambulances, army trucks and fire engines turned the square into a huge, chaotic car park. Flashing blue and red lights colored the statue of the 19th-century King Pedro IV. Rescue workers ran back and forth to help those arriving. They bundled them into ambulances or trucks to take them to hospitals or temporary housing elsewhere in the city. Groups of people huddled under makeshift tarpaulins and covered themselves with blankets.

Behind them, more loud crashing noises came from the area nearer the river. An army officer told Miguel and Antonia that a few buildings had partially collapsed but the rescue workers didn't know exactly how much damage had been done, nor if there were any casualties.

Miguel looked around for the ambulance he needed to pick up the corpses. But he couldn't see it and told the others to wait while he made his way around the swarming square, trying to see through the rain and avoid being knocked down by the emergency vehicles.

Antonia lit a cigarette while she waited, standing beneath a plastic awning over the outside tables at one of the many restaurants lining the square. Amid the noise, Antonia was quiet and pensive. Memories of Brigitte and Katja gripped her – their cooking, walking their dogs on the beach, laughing around a campfire when Antonia tried to sing a cowboy song.

Miguel returned, directing an ambulance that was coming slowly behind him. The policemen lifted the bodies into it and it slowly negotiated its way through the noisy clutter of emergency vehicles and crews dashing around.

"Shall we go?" Miguel said, leaning close to Antonia. "I don't think we'll find anything else here tonight."

"Maybe not," she said, as they walked through the rain and the chaos. But her investigator's mind was already hard at work.

Chapter 2

Antonia walked in her pajamas with her morning coffee onto the veranda of her apartment and looked out over the Baixa. The torrential rain of the previous night had stopped, but the sky was a murky grey.

From where she was living, in a borrowed apartment on Lisbon's highest hill, just outside the walls of St. George's Castle, she could look across the city's terracotta roofs towards the Tagus River and the bridge that looked just like San Francisco's Golden Gate.

But Antonia was restless and in no mood to enjoy the view. She had slept badly, her mind repeatedly casting back to the crime scene and memories of her dead friends. She turned on her iPad and sat down, placing her mug on the table. She went straight to the summary of the local daily papers she received by email.

Brigitte and Katja were front-page news. They were given more prominence than a few dark photographs of last night's chaos, which had happened too late for the morning papers. Antonia started clicking on some of the front pages, pausing to sip her coffee as they loaded. One of the tabloids had got hold of passport photographs of the two women. Their crime reporter's got good police contacts, Antonia thought to herself.

She looked at her friends' impassive faces in the photos. They had been taken quite a few years ago – their hair was different and they looked almost girlish.

Antonia recognized their eyes best. She saw that mixture of hardness and softness that had made them so determined and fearless in their refusal to hide their love for each other. A lesbian relationship like theirs didn't go down well with some people in Germany and Portugal, but they had been undaunted. Antonia had admired their courage and devotion to each other.

The news stories didn't have much to say about the dead women themselves. The Portuguese clearly had a bigger worry, and it was summed up in one of the tabloids' shock-horror headlines in half-page block capitals: "TOURIST KILLER ON THE LOOSE IN LISBON?"

It turned out that a French woman tourist had been found floating in the Tagus the previous week. She had been stabbed, the paper said, but her murder was initially regarded as a tragic one-off incident. Now, with more foreign women found dead, the tabloid speculation was all about a possible serial killer, or maybe even a copycat.

The latest deaths of foreigners had sent the authorities into a panic, the paper said, because bad publicity could ruin the tourist industry – a vital source of revenue for the ailing Portuguese economy. Some 13 million holidaymakers came to Portugal every year. Tourism accounted for about 10 per cent of GDP and, one way or another, kept eight per cent of the working population in jobs. The government was terrified at the prospect of losing that kind of business.

Antonia suspected the newspaper had already had the story in the works before the previous evening's deaths, because it contained lots of convenient and pithy quotes from tourism officials. "The police and the government have got to solve these crimes without delay," said one travel operator. "We can't have a tourist killer rampaging through Lisbon. It'll be the end of us and the end of all the jobs we provide."

How stupid, Antonia thought to herself – Brigitte and Katja weren't even tourists. And anyway, they were tough women and could have fought off a pack of the most determined tourist killers.

But the digital editions of other newspapers were already updating their morning stories with the tourist killer angle, and radio and television coverage was swinging the same alarmist way. The media herd was starting to stampede.

Websites also had close-up photos of the emergency crews in the dark, wet square. The papers spoke of calamity and catastrophe in the old downtown district, and drew the inevitable comparisons with the momentous 1755 Lisbon earthquake and the post-disaster rebuilding. In the end, though, flooding in that part of town surprised nobody.

Antonia sighed, turned off her iPad and went back inside. The apartment was pretty bare. She had been in it for months since she returned to Portugal in the spring. She kept telling herself she would only stay one more month, but it never worked out like that. Her Aunt Fatima and Uncle Alvaro wanted to rent it out, though, so she'd have to find her own place sooner or later. They kept telling her not to worry about it, but she knew everyone was being especially kind and gentle with her. They looked upon her as still being in convalescence, even though it was more than a year since she had been shot.

She was still digesting her move back to 'The Old Country,' though, and all the emotional turmoil of the past year, as well as coming back into contact with Miguel, and wasn't in the mood for house-hunting. She much more fancied getting her teeth into a meaty investigation. And this one was personal.

So much didn't make sense, Antonia thought as she went into her bedroom to get dressed. Could Brigitte and Katja really have "fallen" off the tower? Surely not. A suicide pact? No, it didn't fit. A hit-and-run? Crumpled up like that together, unlikely. And what were two country girls who hated cities doing in Lisbon? Then there was all that flooding and pandemonium and buildings collapsing. What was all that about?

Antonia mulled these things over as she got dressed in her bedroom. She was due at a barbecue lunch for her Aunt Fatima's birthday next to the beach in Caparica, across the river. She decided to dress demurely, since the older generation of her wider family was going to be there. They had come of age under Antonio Salazar's dictatorship and, though they broadly supported the 1974 Carnation Revolution that brought democracy to Portugal, their cultural tastes were conservative. It was a world away from America, where she had spent her formative years and grown into a woman.

Antonia put on a black turtle-neck sweater and black trousers, wrapped a light pink scarf around her neck and tied her hair in a ponytail. She checked herself in the full-length mirror. The dark clothes showed off her curvy figure. She suddenly remembered Brigitte, in Aljezur all those months ago, giving an admiring wolf whistle when she came across Antonia getting dressed. Antonia noticed the glint in Brigitte's eyes – the giveaway that her relationship with Katja went beyond being just friends. It seemed so long ago.

*

The full scale of the damage in downtown Lisbon was still unclear, and Mario Goncalves worried about what to tell his superiors. As deputy public works minister, almost all the tough and delicate decisions fell on him. The minister, his boss, did the nice stuff – cutting ribbons on new buildings, attending banquets, that sort of thing – and left the heavy lifting to him.

Information on the structural soundness of the Baixa's buildings was incomplete and out of date by about 20 years. Even so, Goncalves had to decide, and swiftly, what should be done with the three ministries (justice, agriculture and finance), city hall and the supreme court, which all had their offices there. What he did know was that the basements and ground floors of the ministries were either under water or severely damaged, that there was partial damage to the foundations, and that the damp was eating away at files, documents and computers. This is a nightmare, Mario thought. A large chunk of the financial information pertaining to the country's bailout was at the finance ministry, and its loss would be a political calamity.

Then there was the financial cost. Physically moving all the stuff and getting temporary premises to house the staff and paperwork of the ministries would be costly. The government had little cash to spare for such unanticipated expenses. He would need to do some creative accounting.

"So, what the hell do I tell the PM, Mario?" the minister had screamed at him early in the morning. "You better have a plan ready quickly, or heads will roll."

The minister had put Mario in charge of the entire plan – finding a temporary location for staff to work, as well as funding and the planning for the physical move. Mario, sitting alone at his desk later, put his head in his hands. His words echoed those uttered at the time of the 1755 earthquake, which he had studied at length. "God has forsaken us," he groaned.

*

The Lisbon police headquarters were in a sober 1950s building close to the business district. Wolfgang stepped out of his chauffeured German embassy Mercedes-Benz and, talking on his cellphone, strode through the main gate. Inside, at the reception desk, he showed his ID and clipped the visitor's badge onto his tailored dark suit. Wolfgang's ramrod posture, strong build and no-nonsense demeanor drew some jokey remarks from staff, but not to his face.

Wolfgang ignored the lifts where others were waiting and bounded up the four flights of stairs to the meeting rooms for senior staff. He knocked on the door of Meeting Room 2 and went in. The plain-clothed policemen inside stood up as he entered. There was Miguel and two of his colleagues, Artur and Fernando, and his boss, *Inspector-Chefe* Jorge Braga, who went over to Wolfgang with his hand extended.

"Hello, Mr. Müller, or should I say, *Herr* Muller," he said.

"*Sprechen Sie Deutsch?*" Wolfgang asked, smiling.

"Ha, ha, no, no," Braga said, as Miguel and his colleagues rolled their eyes at each other. Their boss had risen through the ranks due to political patronage, and his lack of aptitude for police work meant he had few friends among those below him.

"I speak English," Wolfgang said. "I am afraid Portuguese is still very difficult for me. I have been here only 15 months."

"Yes, we say Portuguese is a very *traicoeira* language," Braga said and looked at Miguel to help him out with a translation.

"Treacherous," Miguel said.

"*Sim*, exactly," Braga said. "Are you liking Portugal? Where did you go so far?"

"Oh, I've had a good look around," Wolfgang said. "You have a very pretty country. It is a shame it is not better known. I think tourism could be your big future here. And of course I love the food."

"Ha, ha, yes, it is very good," Braga said. "Well, shall we sit down and look at our liaison plan?"

"I have to report directly to the ambassador and to Berlin," Wolfgang said, taking his seat and getting straight down to business. "German media already know about the women's deaths – murders, I should say – and are demanding answers, in my country and in yours. Tourist killings are usually big news. Journalists will soon be prowling around."

"They're the same everywhere," Miguel said. "We'll need to coordinate and keep a tight lid on things."

"We will catch the killer, don't worry," Braga said to Wolfgang.

"I can provide you with information from my side," Wolfgang said. "We are more than happy to share what we know."

"Excellent, excellent," Braga said.

"We're still waiting for the autopsy results," Miguel said. "That's the main thing from our side. How about their IDs?"

"We are trying to trace their relatives," Wolfgang said. "But it seems they, how do you say, dropped out. The last reports put them in Frankfurt. My people are on it."

"Excellent, excellent," Braga said.

"Artur and Fernando have been compiling what we know so far, which isn't much," Miguel said, taking a thin file from Artur and handing it to Wolfgang.

"You two will make an excellent team," Braga said, looking from Miguel to Wolfgang. "Like Benfica!"

Miguel and his colleagues audibly groaned, while Wolfgang smiled graciously.

"I am sure we will, Chief Inspector," Wolfgang said.

"Excellent, excellent," Braga said, shaking Wolfgang's hand. "I am sure we will meet again."

Braga went out, and Miguel turned to Wolfgang.

"So have you dried out yet?" Miguel asked.

"Yes, what a crazy storm," Wolfgang said. "Such a beautiful part of town ruined, I fear. It reminds me of when my brother's town near Bonn was flooded once. They lost just about everything. In the end my brother just sold what he had and moved on. It was the smartest thing to do."

"Well, there's time yet to salvage things. Our best people are on it," Miguel said.

"I hope so," Wolfgang said. He looked at his watch. "How about we go for a beer, get to know each other – in the interest of European police cooperation, of course. I'm buying."

Artur and Fernando appeared eager but they looked to Miguel for a yes or no.

"Sure," Miguel said. "Let's get our coats."

As Miguel's colleagues left the room, Wolfgang took Miguel to one side.

"I have a friend at Europol," Wolfgang said. "There's nothing concrete yet, but he says we ought to consider the possibility of drugs being involved. You know, the Aljezur connection."

"How did you know about Aljezur? You don't waste any time," Miguel said. "Well, yes, unfortunately Portugal is known as a drug gateway to Europe, and it's largely because of that whole coastline down there that's not got enough proper surveillance. It used to be cannabis from North Africa they offloaded on the beaches – there are plenty of remote inlets down there. Now it's cocaine from Latin America that comes through West Africa. We have former colonies there and lots of African emigrants who came over."

"Yes, so I understand," Wolfgang said. "It is something for us to keep in mind."

"Absolutely," Miguel said, "though it's not our first line of investigation at the moment. We have to check out this tourist killer angle first. That has been made our top priority."

"Yes, yes, of course," Wolfgang said. "I'm sorry, I didn't mean to meddle."

"No sweat," Miguel said. "Let's go and have that cold beer. I could really use one."

"Be my guest," Wolfgang said, holding open the door.

*

Antonia set off in her car for Caparica, heading along the narrow, cobbled streets of Alfama where she lived before reaching the broad riverside avenues that led to the bridge. The view from here, with Lisbon on one side and the huge Statue of Christ on the other bank, its arms open towards the city, always made her feel exhilarated.

After 30 minutes of navigating the anarchic traffic she approached Caparica, the seaside town at the head of a 20-kilometer stretch of golden beaches. The town itself was disheveled and seedy, but she continued along the coast until she pulled up at the small beachside villa she remembered from her childhood holidays.

She was met at the gate by three small dogs whose yapping brought her Uncle Alvaro into the front garden.

"Antonia!" he shouted. "My beautiful niece! Everyone will be so glad you're here!"

He was right. As he led Antonia into the back, where the barbecue was smoking beneath the bushy overhead vines, two dozen family members crowded around her. Most were cousins who each had several children. Her cheeks were covered in kisses. Antonia kept laughing and smiling through the barrage. Young nephews – some of whom she had never seen, others she didn't immediately recognize because she hadn't seen them for years – came up to her, most of them keen for details about life in America.

Nobody at the party knew about what had happened the previous night, and Antonia wasn't keen on letting them know and answering all their questions. She wasn't even sure at the moment what the answers were.

Her cousin Susana approached her and took Antonia's hands in hers. She gave Antonia a warm smile and looked fondly into her eyes. Susana had been to visit Antonia several times in the States, though not in recent years.

"Hi, Antonia," Susana said. "How are you keeping? You look good. I heard you'd recovered."

"Yeah, I'm fine. All patched up. It's a bit strange to be back, though. I'm still finding my feet. No job or anything. I'm living in a borrowed apartment..."

Susana suddenly looked troubled.

"What's wrong?" Antonia asked.

"Oh, it's nothing. Well, actually, that's not true. Thing are pretty bad, really."

"How come?"

"I'm sure you've heard how bad things are around here. Eduardo's been laid off. I've had my pay cut at the council. Everything's gone up in price with the new taxes. You know, and the kids..."

Susana's voice trailed off and she bowed her head. Antonia put her arm around her. She hated this feeling of powerlessness, this seeing your family suffering and not being able to do anything except rage against the injustice.

The party was gathering pace, though, and people came over insisting Antonia and Susana pick up a plate and a glass and tuck in. The red wine served in jugs was so strong it was a shade of purple. The women diluted it with lemonade to make an impromptu sangria. Fat sardines sprinkled with rock salt were thrown onto the barbecue, next to thinly-cut pork steaks marinated overnight in garlic, white wine and paprika.

The conversation meandered through the usual subjects – Antonia's return to Portugal and her convalescence, the financial crisis gripping Portugal and the hardship it had brought for families whose pay and pensions were being cut while the cost of living rose. Then, of course, there was the latest football news, which brought raised voices and much gesticulating from the men. Uncle Alvaro started dancing a jig, expertly balancing a grilled sardine on a slice of bread in one hand and a glass of wine in the other – and not spilling a drop.

A distant cousin of Antonia's, who was feeling the effects of the wine, started trying to chat her up.

"You want to come up to my village next weekend? We're killing a pig. It'll be good fun," he said.

"Right," Antonia said. "So you're inviting me to a medieval party, where a bunch of blokes drag a squealing pig onto a table in the middle of the village, while a bunch of other blokes get boozed up and watch, then you stab it in the neck, drain its blood out into bowls to make sausages, then hang it up and cut out its insides – more sausages – then sit around putting cuts of pork on the barbecue and getting completely drunk?"

The cousin thought for a second. "Yeah," he said.

"That's disgusting!" Antonia said. "What would you say if I invited you to an abattoir for a few drinks?"

"Er, well, I suppose I'd say yes," he said.

Miguel came to her rescue. He walked into the party, drawing everybody's attention as the cry went up "Miguel!" As an old friend of the family who grew up around the house in Caparica, he was treated like another son. He went around giving kisses and handshakes and helping himself to wine and a grilled steak sandwich. He ended up alongside Antonia, and they moved over to one side of the patio. The others all noticed and either winked to each other or smiled knowingly.

"What's new?" Antonia asked.

"We're looking for a tourist killer," Miguel said in a low voice.

"What? You're kidding!"

"Well, let's not jump to conclusions," Miguel said defensively.

"I don't buy it," Antonia said. "That's just sensationalist bullshit they serve up in the papers."

"These things are decided at a higher level than me. I'm just a gumshoe on a civil servant's wage. This time it's gone even higher up – the government's all over it, too, what with the tourism stuff and all."

"Well, if you want to go down that road, good luck, but it sounds like amateur hour," Antonia said, turning away.

"Look," Miguel said, his frustration about his life welling up inside him. "I'm the police detective here, not you. You were always going off doing your own thing. You've retired and I'm the cop now, I'm the one in charge, right? So you'll just have to keep your nose out and keep your opinions to yourself, won't you?"

Antonia swiveled sharply and put her face up against his. "Make me," she said.

At that point Aunt Fatima, whose 70th birthday they were celebrating, came over and put a hand on each of them. "You two were always so competitive," she said, "always fighting when you were kids. But you were always so fond of each other. Come on, learn to live with your differences. Life's too short."

Their tempers cooled amid Aunt Fatima's calming presence and kindly demeanor, and the pair of them looked down at their feet like sheepish children.

"I've got to go," Miguel said. "Duty calls. As usual."

"I'll come with you," Antonia said, putting her drink down and picking up her handbag.

Miguel didn't bother trying to stop her. He didn't say so but he was glad to have her company. And there was something he needed to tell her, in private. Antonia, too, was keen to stay close to the investigation. They said their farewells and headed out to their cars.

As they stepped out onto the pavement and the breeze coming off the Atlantic, Antonia grabbed Miguel's arm.

"You haven't told me everything, have you?"

Miguel took out his car keys. "No," he said, bracing himself for the awful details he was about to reveal. "Thing is, they were tortured. Fingernails, you know."

A look of anguish flashed in Antonia's eyes and she stopped in her tracks. "Tortured? What sort of sadistic bastard would do that to them?"

"That's not all," Miguel went on, wishing he could break the news more easily but knowing Antonia would want it given to her straight. "They were raped, too. And they were still alive – barely – when they hit the ground." He added, hoping to ease her pain: "They were probably unconscious, though."

Antonia looked at him, her mind working through the possibilities. "So you think they were thrown off the tower?"

"Looks like it. Or from another building. It explains the extent of the physical damage. And I doubt they jumped."

"No," Antonia said, sounding thoughtful. "They wouldn't have."

Antonia stared out to sea, deep in thought. Her resolve to find out what happened to Brigitte and Katja hardened.

"Have you checked CCTV footage around there?" Antonia asked.

"Of course. There isn't any of that spot."

"Of the scene itself? But what about the surrounding area. Something must have been picked up somewhere."

Miguel looked sheepish. "Yes, well, that's our next line of inquiry." Antonia knew him well enough to know when he was lying.

"You follow me," Miguel said, getting into his car and hoping to change the subject away from his oversight. He was keen to move on from the bad news that had been troubling him all the way on the drive over. "We'll drop your car at your place, then go on."

"Where to?"

"Wolfgang called. He's been digging around for us. Sounds like he's found something, but he wouldn't say on the phone."

*

Miguel and Antonia saw Wolfgang waiting at the corner, down the street from the embassy.

"He's wearing his flashy businessman's suit again," Antonia said. She couldn't help associating Wolfgang with Portugal's bailout and the economic misery that had come with it, which she believed rich countries like Germany had masterminded and which had brought so much hardship. The unemployment rate had risen close to 20 percent, and it was 35 percent among people under 25. The spending cuts were madness. How could anyone remain unmoved?

"It might be best if you let him sit in the passenger's seat," Miguel said. Antonia looked daggers at him, forcing Miguel to add, "He is the official liaison after all. And he's been a big help."

Antonia reluctantly got out of the car when they pulled up and gave Wolfgang a cool look as she opened the back door. Miguel knew she was cut up about what he'd told her. Antonia had a famously quick temper, and he worried she might take it out on Wolfgang.

"Hi, Wolfgang," Miguel shouted from inside the car.

Wolfgang bent over to see inside. "Hello, Miguel. How was your lunch in beautiful Caparica – one of my favorite places?"

"It was good, thanks. Shame about the gray sky, though."

Wolfgang turned to Antonia, who was leaning on the car and staring coldly at him. "This is official business," Wolfgang said. "You will not be joining with us, no?"

"Not in the biblical sense, no," Antonia said. "But then, you're not a Portuguese cop either, are you? In fact, your jurisdiction, if you have any, is about 2,000 kilometers northeast of here."

"It's all right, Wolfgang," Miguel said from inside the car. "Let's all go. Three heads are better than one. We've all got something to contribute."

Wolfgang and Antonia got into the car. Wolfgang handed a piece of paper to Miguel. "We will be going there directly please," he said. "This is the address."

"What's there?" Miguel asked.

"This is the place where the dead women were staying."

"Wow," Miguel said. "How did you find this?"

"I am connected very well."

"Right," said Antonia from the back seat, lowering the window and taking out a cigarette.

Miguel pulled into the traffic and they headed across the hilly city. Miguel and Wolfgang chatted about Portugal, its wine and food, its pretty countryside and friendly people. Wolfgang appeared to know Portugal pretty well, though he'd barely been in the country for more than a year. Antonia didn't say a word.

On their way they drove past the cordoned-off downtown district. Looking down towards the river, Antonia and Miguel could see emergency crews with heavy machinery milling around the flooded area. "Good grief," Miguel said, "what a mess. That's going to take some sorting out." Wolfgang continued to stare straight ahead.

Antonia leaned forward and spoke into Wolfgang's ear.

"So, Wolfie," she said, "do you wear black as a sign of mourning for the dying Portuguese economy and the massed ranks of unemployed?"

Miguel shifted uneasily in his seat and pretended to be paying attention to the traffic.

"We make our bed, as you say, and then we lie down in it," Wolfgang said. "In life, there are strivers and slackers."

"Ah yes," Antonia said. "How true. But I would go further than that. I would say there are hateful, despicable strivers who live a life of tedium and take their revenge on those who are having fun, and then there are the delightful slackers who appreciate the good things in life and find the strivers hilariously misguided and pathetic."

Wolfgang didn't flinch. "The German people know your suffering," he said. "We also have suffered, you must not forget. In the 1920s our economy was destroyed. There were more than 4 trillion Deutschmarks to the dollar. Millions had no food. My parents remembered it. They had hard times. For that reason we are very careful to make the euro a strong currency, with rules – for the good of everyone."

"Hold on there, Wolfie," Antonia said, taking a drag on her cigarette. "The way I got taught history, austerity didn't work in Germany between the wars, so after World War Two Americans pumped money into your country and that allowed you to become wealthy. But now you want austerity for us. Do you think that'll work?"

"We must follow the rules."

"Even if they bring hardship that's difficult to comprehend in 21st century western Europe?" Antonia asked. "I don't think you've seen the suffering I've seen, even in my own family."

"We are helping you, no?" Wolfgang said. "We give you billions. We cannot give you the fruits of our labor without some reward, after all. It's the way of the world. But all we get is people asking for more. We also must take care of our own."

"You like giving orders, you mean. Come to that, you like obeying them too."

"Knock it off, Antonia," Miguel said, glancing in the rear-view mirror. "We need to work together. Wolfgang's been a big help with the case. There are things you don't know about, things above your head – the German police, Europol and things."

Wolfgang turned around and looked at Antonia. "You are not Portuguese, I am correct? You are an American citizen."

"You've been checking up on me. What a surprise," Antonia said, shaking her head. "My blood is pure Portuguese, for your information. And I'm proud of it. It's better than being--"

"We're here," Miguel interrupted diplomatically. They pulled up outside a block of apartments. "Fifth floor." They all looked up through the car windows.

Chapter 3

Mario Goncalves chewed the fingernails on his left hand as, with his right, he clicked through the emailed reports he was receiving hourly from city engineers. They painted an increasingly grim picture of the scale of the damage underneath the Baixa where the rush of water had weakened foundations holding up thousands of tons of stone and concrete. Centuries-old buildings were fragile and tottering in the waterlogged earth. The experts still weren't even sure if the buildings could be saved. Officials from the Civil Protection Agency had pulled out the heavy machinery and barely dared venture along the streets near the river. Inside the buildings, the basements and ground floors had suffered severe water damage.

Mario's phone didn't stop ringing. His boss was out. He had gone to an official opening of something or other and no doubt would be staying on for another long lunch of rubbing shoulders with the rich and powerful, Mario thought bitterly. Public works was notorious for dodgy building contracts and generous backhanders. A man could set himself up for life, with the right connections.

Just before he went out, the minister had passed by Mario's office. He had remarked that maybe they should just give up on the buildings and shift everything out of the city center. Governments had been talking for years about 'decentralization,' anyway. Maybe this was the moment to actually do it.

"See what you think," Mario's boss said as he pulled on his coat and walked out of the door.

And Mario was thinking. A lot. He was a history buff and he loved the downtown district, which was a short walk away from his office. He liked to stroll along the Baixa's streets, dropping in for his lunch at one of the many cheap restaurants serving traditional Portuguese fare. Fernando Pessoa, Portugal's great 20th-century poet and Mario's favorite writer, used to do the same.

Mario didn't like the idea of spoiling the downtown's classical, distinguished character. It had been Portugal's seat of power since the early 16th century, when the Age of Expansion turned Lisbon into one of the richest cities in the world. Praca do Comercio was still one of Europe's biggest squares. King Manuel I moved his residence down here from St George's Castle in 1511, though his palace was destroyed, like much of Lisbon, in the 1755 quake. In the city's reconstruction, the Marquis of Pombal placed the riverside square at the heart of his recovery plan and installed government offices in the elegant arcades of marble and stone around it.

Now, this prime piece of real estate was a disaster area. The TV set in Mario's office broadcast live pictures from the scene for most of the day. It was the biggest story in years and had pushed everything else off the front pages. No more was heard about a possible tourist killer. Mario sighed and tried to figure out how he could help save a part of his home town he considered a national treasure. So much was at stake.

He clicked on the latest email that had just dropped into his inbox and suddenly stiffened. He buzzed his secretary. "Margarida," he said, "get the boss on the phone, quick."

*

Antonia had just come out of the all-night store where she usually shopped after a late shift when the bullet ripped through her side. The .45 slug came in from the back, piercing her right kidney. Blood spat out from the hole in her belly as the bullet went through. The gunshot punched her with a kinetic blast that span her round and flung her headlong onto the sidewalk, spilling the contents of her brown paper bag onto the dark street. Milk, cornflakes, pizza were strewn around her limp body. Antonia lay paralyzed by shock, vaguely aware of feet on the sidewalk around her and someone calling 911.

She didn't see who fired the shot. Nobody did. A couple of witnesses would later testify they saw a red pick-up speeding away from the scene, but not much more. The storekeeper, who liked having a cop stopping by regularly, was eager to help. But he shrank from repeating the rumor that was being whispered around the Massachusetts town. The cops already knew it anyway.

"I ain't saying nothing 'bout that," Eddie Machado said. The cops had asked if anyone had been acting strangely around Antonia or asking about her. They already knew the answer, but it wasn't something that could be spoken out loud.

Before she slipped into unconsciousness, Antonia thought she was going to die. Emergency surgery saved her life, though not her right kidney.

Her family had talked her into becoming a cop. In that part of Massachusetts, in those years, a government job was a safe bet, a sure thing. The jobs in the local textile mills had gone, sent over to Asia, gift-wrapped.

Antonia's parents had emigrated to the U.S. in 1978, when she was eight and the year when the International Monetary Fund granted Portugal its first of three bailouts over four decades. Spending cuts and other austerity measures, as well as the continuing turmoil after the 1974 Revolution, meant that chances of getting on in life dried up. Her parents had family in Massachusetts. They had gone there from Portugal in the 1950s to escape Salazar's dictatorship and the harassment of his secret police who hunted down dissenters like her beloved grandfather.

The transatlantic move was a horrible wrench for an eight-year-old. She had lived all her short life by the sea, playing many months of the year on the beaches at Caparica, but in America they set up home in an industrial town. She felt desperately awkward at first, like a misfit. America was so big and Portugal was so small. The scale was all wrong. But the feeling didn't last long. Her new hometown had a long Portuguese pedigree. After nearly two centuries in Massachusetts, whose 19th-century whaling industry drew workers from the Azores and Madeira islands, the Portuguese had their own businesses, bars and clubs. And she had plenty of cousins to play with.

Antonia's family worked in the garment industry mills, like the ones in Portugal, but by the time she came of working age the textile companies were limping into the 1990s and laying people off as they struggled to survive.

She had been reluctant at first to consider a career in the local police force. But she wasn't the studying kind, didn't go on to college, and her high-school diploma was enough to get her a job as a patrol officer and a $50,000 a year salary. She hated the police bureaucracy and the departmental politics, so not getting a promotion was fine. And she discovered that being a cop suited her. She was naturally methodical, determined and a hater of injustice, which sparked lots of foot-stamping arguments when she was growing up, especially as she was an only child. The uniform helped tame her rebelliousness.

Even so, she almost gave it all up and moved back to Portugal, a country for which she held a deep fondness. During vacations in Lisbon in her twenties – single and tired of nagging questions about when she was going to get married and start a family – her relationship with Miguel, her childhood friend, had become increasingly tender and affectionate. They were falling in love. He was a policeman and hopeful of making detective. He wanted her to move back to Portugal, but she couldn't get a job with the Lisbon police because she was now an American. In the end, neither of them was willing to sacrifice their career. They broke up and didn't speak for years.

Now here she was, an unmarried cop just turned 40, lying bleeding on the sidewalk with a bullet wound in her gut and her TV dinner all over the sidewalk.

Investigators never found who shot her, nor any motive. But there was no doubt in her mind about what had happened. Antonia had been told to back off when she started asking questions about who was behind an influx of cocaine into the town and the state. Several clues had led her to suspect a group of Latin Americans she mostly saw on her night patrols, though she figured they were just the small fish.

When she delved too deeply into a series of gruesome murders, with bodies dumped in the woods around town, she ran into resistance from senior officers and local politicians. So she started her own unsanctioned investigation. "Do what you think's best, do what you think's right," her grandfather always said. "Don't let anyone knock you off your path."

It wasn't long before she was certain she was on to a modern day Tammany Hall conspiracy funded by Colombian cocaine that she kept encountering in her investigations of small-time crimes. Her on-off boyfriend for the previous three years, Mike Ferreira, a local sheriff's deputy who wanted to marry her, warned her off, too. He said that her snooping was a pointless indulgence, though she remembered that he used more colourful language.

"You're wasting your goddam time," he said. "You're just gonna get yourself into a heap of trouble and lose your goddam job."

"A job isn't the most important thing in life," she shot back at him.

"Tell that to the guy sleeping under the bridge," he said.

The episode made her realize that she and Mike were fundamentally different, and she broke off the relationship.

Days later, she took a bullet. Her determination had cost her a kidney. And a fiance.

Chapter 4

Antonia, Miguel and Wolfgang stood in light drizzle outside the five-storey apartment building. It had been renovated and, in a traditional Lisbon style, painted pale pink with white stone trimming, and it looked out over the river.

"The women were accommodated in the top floor apartment," Wolfgang said. "The building belongs to a Swiss man, Rolf Fankhauser, 36 years old, from a very wealthy family. He is estranged from them, however. He possesses an impressive real estate portfolio. He rents out most of these apartments."

"You're very well informed," Antonia said, giving Miguel a look.

"I'm assuming you've only just found all this out, Wolfgang," Miguel said.

"Oh yes, I telephoned you promptly as I received the information."

"What floor does this Swiss fellow live on?" Miguel asked.

"The first," Wolfgang said, as Antonia pushed at the thick wooden door. It was unlocked and swung open invitingly.

"No wonder I have so many crimes to solve," Miguel said as they went in.

They went up the polished wooden stairs. Traditional Portuguese blue and white tiles lined the walls all the way up the staircase.

"No expense spared," said Miguel.

"Watch you don't make too much noise," Antonia said. "We want to catch him unawares."

"Yes, thank you, Antonia," Miguel said sarcastically.

They stood outside the door of the first-floor apartment. Miguel took out his badge and rapped on the door. They could hear music inside. A wiry man with fair hair and a goatee opened the door. He was wearing an old T-shirt, jeans and was in bare feet.

"Rolf Fankhauser?" Miguel said.

"Yes," Rolf said nervously as he looked at the three of them. He took a wary step backwards.

"Miguel Soares. Police detective." Miguel held up his badge. "I'd like a chat, if we could have a few moments."

"Of course," Rolf said, turning his head and glancing uncertainly around his large living room.

"Can we come in?" Miguel asked.

"Er, yes, sure, sure," Rolf said, backing up.

"This is Antonia Fortunata and Wolfgang Müller," Miguel said. He added, before Rolf could ask who they were, "Just a few questions as part of our inquiry."

"Uh-huh," Rolf said absently as he walked back into the living room rubbing his chin and casting his eyes around.

Wolfgang and Antonia swiftly took in the room, but there wasn't much to see apart from the jumble of hi-tech equipment on a large mahogany desk with a laptop and a thick clump of wires disappearing behind it. Rolf was obviously a minimalist as far as decoration went. There was just a two-person sofa, an armchair and a telescope on a stand pointing out of the picture window. Not even a photograph on the wall.

"It's about two German women," Miguel said, taking out his notebook.

"Oh yeah," Rolf said, sounding half-helpful, half-suspicious.

"They were staying here, I believe," Miguel said, consulting his notebook. "A Brigitte Richter and Katja Hoffmann." He looked at Rolf, gauging his reaction.

"Ah, yes, they are in one of my upstairs apartments."

"No, they're not. They're in the morgue."

Rolf went white. "They're dead?" Miguel, Antonia and Wolfgang watched him in silence. "*Mein Gott*. That's unbelievable. I saw them – I mean, I bumped into them on the stairs just the other day." Rolf went to sit on the armchair. Miguel and Antonia took it as a cue and sat on the sofa. Wolfgang went to sit at the desk.

"What happened?" Rolf asked.

"That's what we're trying to find out," Miguel said. "I need you to tell us everything you can about them – what they did, who they hung out with and so on."

"Well, I don't know," Rolf said. "I mean, I just rent out apartments. Mostly short-term stuff. I don't socialize with people. I'm mostly on my own. They just pay me and then leave."

"So you didn't know them? They weren't friends of yours?"

"Well, no, I mean, I didn't know them. They haven't been here a week. I saw them, they paid me. They have their lives and I have mine."

"'Had,' you mean. They 'had' their lives."

"Oh yes, oh my God, it's just so terrible. I can't believe it," Rolf said, putting his head in his hands.

Wolfgang, taking advantage of Rolf's distraction, surreptitiously lifted open the half-closed laptop lid.

"How did they find this apartment then?" Antonia interjected, prompting a furious glance in her direction from Miguel.

"Well, I mean, people find me. It's word of mouth, really."

"They lived in Aljezur," Miguel said.

Rolf appeared to search his memory. "Ah, yes, maybe from there, a long time ago, maybe that's it."

"You knew them from Aljezur, then," Miguel said, writing in his notebook.

"Well, you know, it's like I say, 'know' is probably too strong a word."

"Did you or did you not know them from Aljezur?" Miguel asked, his tone hardening.

"Yes, all right, you could say that."

"I want you to say it. If it's true."

"Yes, then, I met them in Aljezur." Rolf noticed Wolfgang looking at his laptop. "I don't think you're allowed to do that without a warrant," he said.

"You have my apologies," Wolfgang said, turning back round to the others but leaving the laptop open.

"We're just here to put the facts together. I didn't bring a warrant because I thought you'd want to help," Miguel said.

"Yes, yes, I do," Rolf said nervously. "I just know my rights, that's all."

"Let's get back to the facts then," Miguel said, running his pencil down his notebook.

"Aren't you curious about what happened to them, how they died?" Antonia asked Rolf, prompting Miguel to grind his teeth.

Rolf looked startled. "Yes, yes, of course I am," he said.

Miguel and Antonia sat looking at Rolf, who held their gaze but squirmed in his chair. Wolfgang had quietly gone back to the laptop.

"They were murdered," Miguel said.

There was a moment of tense silence in the room.

"Well, I didn't have anything to do with it," Rolf said, shifting in his chair.

"I didn't suggest you did," Miguel said coolly. There was something about Rolf he didn't like. Maybe it was his wealth. Miguel felt resentful about having to get by with an ever-decreasing standard of living. But it wasn't that. Something else was amiss. He just couldn't put his finger on it yet.

"They lived upstairs, right?"

"Yes, yes, they did. Fourth floor. I haven't seen them for a few days now, though. They haven't been in their apartment," Rolf said, then added quickly: "But I wouldn't know whether they were in there or not. It's all very private here."

"Where were you on Tuesday evening?"

"What?" Rolf replied. "Er, well, let me see. I was here! Here on my own."

"Can anyone vouch for that?"

"No. Like I said, I was on my own."

"Nobody stopped by? Saw you on the stairs or anything?"

"No."

"You sound very sure about that."

"That's because I am," Rolf said, regaining his confidence.

Miguel paused. Then he had a brainwave. "Did you know a French woman called Chantal LeBlanc?"

Rolf looked like he was going to be sick. He tried to compose himself. Looking at the floor, he said, "Yes, she was staying here."

"You know she was found in the river, stabbed to death?"

Rolf gulped. "No, no, I didn't know that. I haven't seen her much either. For quite a while."

Miguel and Antonia stared at Rolf. He tried to stare back, but he couldn't. He got up and went to the window, nervously running his hands through his hair.

"Detective," Wolfgang said. They had almost forgotten he was there. "Come here and look at this," he said, pointing at the laptop screen.

Miguel and Antonia got up and went over. Rolf looked to be in panic. On the computer screen were photos of naked and semi-naked women. Wolfgang kept clicking and new photos appeared. There were lots of them. The women were in an apartment and seemed unaware they were being photographed. Some photos were intimate and left very little to the imagination.

"Hidden cameras in the apartments, I suspect," Wolfgang said.

"Stop!" Antonia shouted. "That's Brigitte and Katja. Oh my God!"

The three of them turned to Rolf. "You disgusting pervert!" Antonia shouted at him.

Rolf was agitated, he couldn't stand still. "I didn't kill anyone! I didn't!"

Miguel strode over to him. Rolf recoiled but Miguel got him by the scruff of the neck and shoved him against the wall. "You're busted, you sick bastard!" Miguel screamed into Rolf's face and threw him to the ground.

Antonia's eyes flared but she fought the urge to assault Rolf. Wolfgang stood back and shook his head. Miguel took out his cellphone and called for a car to come and pick up Rolf.

"It appears that we have our man," Wolfgang said. Turning to Miguel he said, "Please inform me when you obtain a warrant to search the fourth-floor apartment."

Miguel nodded and Wolfgang left the room. Antonia was still upset. She glanced at the computer and felt rage, but she was determined to keep a cool focus on the investigation. She sat down and lit a cigarette and stared at the sky through the picture window while Miguel worked on his notes.

"This is too pat," Antonia said after a while. Miguel looked at her. "He's not big enough to handle the two of them."

"He could have got help. Paid someone. He's not short of money."

"True. But he's just a pervert. My intuition tells me there's more to this."

"Ah yes, female intuition," Miguel said.

Chapter 5

Mario stared intently at the blinking cursor on his computer screen for several minutes until he snapped back into focus.

"Attention Mario Goncalves," the email in front of him read. "For your information, the server (mainframe) computers in the basement of the finance ministry have been destroyed by water. They are no longer functioning."

The implications could be huge. Every little detail of the government's finances was stored on those computers, and the time of year when the administration would prepare the budget was fast approaching. Worse still, all financial information relating to Portugal's bailout, including agreements, amendments and reports, from the European Union and IMF, were also kept there.

This mounting disaster could put a big question mark over the government's ability to abide by the terms of the bailout, Mario thought to himself. That would send a new wave of jitters through international financial markets. Banks would teeter. All hell could break loose, given how nervous investors were.

Mario prayed that there were hard copies of the documents but doubted it. The government hadn't had enough money for cloud computing. Either way, it all just added to the growing scale of the disaster. Mario's job wasn't getting any easier.

The phone on his desk rang as Margarida put her head around the door and gave him that serious look of hers that meant it was the minister on the line. Mario picked up the receiver.

"Now what?" his boss said impatiently.

"Well, it seems the entire finance ministry may not be functioning," said Mario, not wanting to waste any time. "All the servers at the ministry were destroyed in the flooding."

"Oh my God," the minister said. "That could force the whole government to shut down. We're blind without those files!" The minister cursed under his breath. "I'm afraid to say, Mario, you'll have to let the PM's office know. I'm busy. This is part of your job and you'll have to deal with it. There have to be backups somewhere, find them."

It was as if each bit of news that reached Mario was worse than the previous one. Every awful development he feared was playing out and he knew that with each one the moment to call for a full evacuation of downtown government office facilities was drawing closer. He knew he would basically have to make the decision himself and, what's more, he knew his boss wanted it that way to avoid any potential blame – it was always like that with the minister. But first he had to inform the prime minister's office of the latest development.

"Margarida, can you get me the PM's deputy on the line, please," he said quickly through the half-open door.

Margarida couldn't help but admire her boss but she worried about the strain he was under. She could see the worry and the fatigue etching lines in his youthful face. She was the only one who fully knew how much responsibility he actually had, and as each day of the crisis passed she resented the minister more for placing this heavy burden on her boss. She placed the call to the prime minister's office.

"Hello Jose, I'm calling with an update," said Mario to the deputy prime minister who he knew slightly. "I'm afraid it's not good news."

"Hi Mario, so what is this latest bad news?" said Jose.

"All the servers at the finance ministry are down, all data is gone," said Mario simply, knowing any sugar coating would just be counter-productive.

"Oh God," said Jose before his voice trailed off into silence for a few moments.

Then Jose regained his composure and any element of friendship in his voice completely disappeared.

"You know what that means, right Mario? What the fuck are we supposed to do now?" he said.

"We need to find backups as soon as possible," said Mario hopefully.

"Yeah well, that's easy for you to say," Jose snapped back. "That's if there are any backups. Okay, Mario, this is what I want you to do. Keep this completely under wraps until I get back to you. The press would have a field day with this, and the PM is deeply concerned."

At that moment Mario realized for the first time that he had become a pawn in an increasingly dangerous political game. It was clear that the risks were extremely high and rising. How the government handled the crisis would decide its future. And his. Still, he felt a duty to play it straight and decided to grab the bull by the horns.

"You know Jose, we may be fast approaching the point when we have to decide whether to evacuate the whole Baixa. It might not be safe. The buildings' foundations have been weakened," he said. "I think you need to think about it, at least to consider it and make the prime minister aware of the possibility."

"Mario, I am completely stunned by what you just said. To even consider such a possibility would be like a defeat," said Jose, hiding his growing concerns behind anger.

"Anyway, with the information you have just given me, how would we finance an evacuation, with money from which budget? Where would we put everyone, everything? Have you imagined what it would involve? God, it makes my head spin just to think about it. Let's just keep it simple, shall we, and take one step at a time," Jose said and hung up.

Mario walked over to the window and looked down at the downtown district, with its priceless historic buildings, churches, squares and cobble-stone streets. He wondered whether it would still be there when his young children grew up.

*

A police car pulled up outside the apartment building to take Rolf away. Miguel had put plastic cuffs on him and kept him sitting on a chair while they waited. Miguel and Antonia sat staring at him, shaming him into looking away. Wolfgang had left, appearing very pleased with himself and saying he must inform his superiors of the latest developments without delay.

Miguel and Antonia picked up Rolf, each holding one of his arms, and marched him down the flight of stairs to the building's main entrance and the waiting patrol car.

"You don't know half of what's going on in this city," Rolf said to Miguel as they lowered him into the car. "I know what's going on. But I'm not telling you."

Miguel resisted the urge to slap Rolf around the head. He slammed the door and muttered "pervert" under his breath.

Antonia and Miguel decided to walk down the cobble-stone street to grab a coffee. Everything was nearby in the downtown district, and as they walked they could see the top of the Santa Justa tower, where the girls had fallen to their deaths.

"I just can't get Brigitte and Katja out of my head," Antonia said as they sat down on bar stools at a cafe. "There is definitely more to this."

Miguel looked intently at her as she spoke, thinking that he was really liking the time they were spending together. She was funny and chatty, everything his dour wife was not.

"What do you think Miguel?" she asked, interrupting his thoughts. He didn't know why Brigitte and Katja were in Lisbon. Antonia did. Maybe she should tell him, she thought.

"Well actually, I'd love to spend more time with you not just talking about the case all the time," he said, looking into her eyes and failing in his attempt to make it sound like a joke.

"Oh, come on Miguel, we've been over all this, just leave it, will you," she said.

"I just really enjoy your company, that's all."

"That's all well and good but first, you are actually married and second, I don't think it's a good idea anyway," she said, leaning over the bar counter to get the waiter's attention.

"On the first point, yes you are technically right, but frankly it doesn't feel like much of a marriage these days," he said.

"What does that mean?" she said.

"I think she's sleeping with somebody else," he said, hitting a raw nerve in Antonia. She didn't want a relationship with Miguel but she sure didn't want him to suffer the humiliation of his wife cheating on him either.

"I'm really sorry to hear that Miguel," she said. "But surely the first thing you should do is try to talk to her, to see if you have something that can be saved."

"I guess you're right, we'll see how it goes."

Antonia's concentration and commitment were part of what made her a good cop. Despite Miguel's confession about his wife, all Antonia really wanted was to focus on the case.

"Please, can we just get back to business – the deaths of Brigitte and Katja?" she said.

Miguel was momentarily lost in his thoughts as he wondered how things would have been with his wife if he had a different job. But he realized there was no point in talking about it with Antonia. He had probably already confessed too much to her. He could see she didn't want to get any closer to him emotionally while he was still married, however bad that marriage was. He decided to stick to the case.

"Yeah, I suppose there are still some loose ends," he said. "I guess now we just have to wait for them to question Rolf and then get a warrant to search Brigitte and Katja's apartment to take things further."

"I still think it's all just too easy," she said. "Something's fishy. We've got to keep at it."

Miguel had now listened to such comments from Antonia for a few days and even if he was falling for her, she was seriously stepping on his toes. It was beginning to annoy him and made him think back to her comments about Aljezur – he wondered if she had told him everything.

"Antonia, you keep saying these things about the investigation even though you are not actually part of it," he said, thinking how she had virtually told him nothing about her meeting with the two women in Aljezur.

"I mean, what did you mean with your comment that there is probably more to this, that Rolf doesn't look like he did it?" he said. "How do you know, or more importantly, is there something you know that I don't?"

Antonia was taken aback at his sudden switch from a confessing cuckold to angry cop. But he was right, she was withholding information. She hadn't told him earlier because she didn't want to share it with Wolfgang. But now she had no choice.

"Okay, I'm really sorry but yeah there is something I didn't tell you about the women," she said. "They had suspicions about something going on here in Lisbon."

"Thanks a hell of a lot Antonia," Miguel said, sarcastically. "This will do wonders for our mutual trust, I'm sure. Well, what exactly is it?"

Antonia took a sip of her coffee and remembered the fear and excitement in Brigitte and Katja's eyes on the beach in Aljezur when they told her of their suspicions. They didn't say much but it was certainly enough to shed an entirely new light on their brutal killings.

"Their exact words were that they were onto something big in Lisbon and that they didn't want to tell me the details because it could put my life at risk," Antonia said.

Miguel was furious. "Do you not realize that by not telling me you were breaking the law? That's called hampering a police investigation! I could arrest you!"

Antonia looked away.

"The world doesn't revolve around you, you know," Miguel said. He took a deep breath and tried to calm down. "It only changes the entire case by suggesting a credible motive for possible murder."

"I suppose it does," Antonia said coolly. "So, now what?"

Miguel felt like telling her to stay out of the case altogether. But she gave him one of her soft, apologetic smiles and he knew he didn't have the heart to push her away.

He took a sip of his coffee. "I guess we need to go to Aljezur," he said.

Antonia was instantly hit with mixed emotions at going back to the carefree beach town. She remembered the three weeks she spent there early in the summer – she had been able to let go, be free and escape from her worries in front of the evening bonfires and on the golden beaches with the hippies who had welcomed her like close friends. But it would be tough going back without Brigitte and Katja there.

Chapter 6

It was a beautiful, crisp autumn day with blue skies when Miguel picked up Antonia the next morning. They crossed the bridge over the Tagus River and headed south out of Lisbon on the highway, down Portugal's spine. They didn't talk much. A sense of calm descended on Antonia as they drove through the Alentejo region with its enchanting cork forests, olive groves and rolling plains. Miguel felt somber and didn't feel like chatting after his blurted confession about his wife.

They arrived early afternoon in Aljezur's snug beach cove. It was bright and clear, and the Atlantic, calm now, sparkled in the sun as it washed up on the broad beach. The small resort town had a spectacular setting among the cliffs along Portugal's west coast, just north of where the country bends around to the Algarve tourist region. Antonia and Miguel checked into a hostel and headed for a seaside restaurant.

"It's just like I remember it," Antonia said as they sat down in front of a large window looking straight down at the beach. "Except Brigitte and Katja aren't here," she added sadly. They ordered grilled fish, the spectacularly fresh kind, straight out of the sea that Antonia had longed for ever since she left Aljezur in the summer.

"Yeah, and it's full of hippies too," said Miguel, never having been especially impressed by those who chose to duck out of the responsibilities of life, as he saw it. "But since you know the place, how do you think we should go about this?"

She hadn't thought about it much, perhaps because she didn't want to make her friends suspects in the investigation. But she had to, she owed it to Brigitte and Katja.

"Perhaps the best would be if I approach them first, as a friend," she said. "I could go this evening, then we can take it from there."

"Okay, that's a plan, but keep your mind on the investigation please," said Miguel. "This is a big case and I can't afford any cock-ups, we don't have any warrants."

"Don't worry Miguel, I'll tread carefully, I promise not to mess up," she said with a sly glint in her eye.

They finished lunch and returned to the hostel along the town's cobbled streets.

*

Antonia remembered the path along the dunes to her friends' camp well. Its makeshift tents and tepees nestled between the beach and Aljezur's official camp site. Local authorities had never done anything about it, though it was in the protected environmental area on the edge of the beach. The hippies didn't bother anybody, so nobody bothered them. Antonia gulped deep breaths of the sea air. Seagulls flew overhead as she walked along the path at sunset. Looking out across the ocean, she thought that over the horizon was America, but she pushed the thought out of her mind.

She had dressed down, put on jeans and a baggy jumper, to look the part of the returning friend. They knew she had been a cop back in the United States but had no idea of her involvement in Brigitte and Katja's murder case. She hoped to get all the information she needed without even involving Miguel.

Dieter stood in the entrance to his tepee when Antonia walked into the camp. She smiled when she saw him and he smiled back and they hugged. He looked the same as he had a few months ago, with his long blond hair, beads around his neck and flowery shirt. He was a nice German, unlike Wolfgang, she thought.

"What a nice surprise, *Mein Schatz*," he said, gently stroking her arm with that warmth she adored. "What brings you here?"

She struggled to find the right words as she looked over at Brigitte and Katja's tent, nestled behind Dieter's small ornamental garden of cannabis plants and orange and olive Bonsai trees. Antonia decided to not say a thing about the investigation and hope for the best.

"I just needed a break for a couple of days from Lisbon," she said. "And I couldn't think of a better place to come than here. I also heard about Brigitte and Katja. I feel so sad. Maybe that's why I wanted to come."

"It was a complete shock, those two lovely women who had struggled so hard to find happiness," said Dieter, looking momentarily dejected. "Their spirits live on in all of us."

She saw the pain in his eyes, his sadness at how incomprehensible their deaths were to him and the others in their peaceful community.

"What actually happened to them?" she said, as the cop in her returned.

"It was all horrendous, we just don't understand why," said Dieter. "It seems they may have been killed but the authorities haven't told us anything, we aren't family."

"I just saw the headlines in the papers, it was an incredible shock," said Antonia. "I don't understand what they were involved in."

"I'm not sure, I just don't want to think about it," he said, pulling himself together. "Let's not talk about it. You should just enjoy being here. It's so nice to see you! We're having a party on the beach tonight, you must come."

She felt it was best to stop asking him about Brigitte and Katja. She looked over to their little tent and decided to see how the evening developed instead.

As the sun set, members of the community of hippies came and went around the sandy paths that ran between the camp's tents and communal areas, carrying wood and preparing for the barbecue on the beach in the evening. There were about 50 of them in the camp. Most were Germans, but there were Dutch and Portuguese there too. There was also a man called Moriba from Guinea-Bissau, the former Portuguese colony in West Africa. He kept mostly to himself and occasionally vanished for days on end before returning to the camp, so Antonia never really got to know him very well. Nobody paid him much attention but he was always fun and cheerful when he was around. All those in the community had been drawn to a carefree lifestyle in warm southern Europe, surfing and living off the land. It felt like a million miles away from the urban grime of capital cities.

Dieter invited Antonia into his tepee for some tea and they spent an hour chatting before heading to the beach to join the others. At this time of year, the setting sun cast long, beautiful shadows around the pine trees and tents in the camp as a sort of magical haze drifted in the air from the salt water spray off the sea.

It was already dark when Antonia and Dieter walked down the path, which was lit up by torches along the way to the beach where they could see the flames of the bonfire dancing into the night sky. People sat around the bonfire, playing the guitar and singing and drinking beer. Antonia swayed a bit to an old Janis Joplin song she heard them play and then spotted Anja and Heike – two of Brigitte and Katja's best friends – sitting on a log next to the fire. She rushed over to them.

"Hi girls," she said as she approached from behind the log. "Surprise!"

They turned around and jumped up to hug their returning friend.

"Hi Antonia, why didn't you tell us you were coming," Anja said. "It's great to see you."

"I just decided last minute to come down, I needed some time off from Lisbon," Antonia said.

"Well, it's lovely either way," Heike said.

Heike and Anja were another lesbian couple and had been Brigitte and Katja's closest friends. The four of them were like family and they had been unusually kind to Antonia, letting her into their circle despite not belonging to it. Antonia knew that if anybody had any more knowledge about what Brigitte and Katja were doing in Lisbon it was them. They were the best possible chance she had, so she had to be patient and smart. She sat down with them and started chatting, small talk at first, as the smell of joints mixed with smoke from the bonfire wafted around them.

"So, how are you, how is the bead industry doing?" Antonia said, remembering their meager livelihood.

"Well, so-so, I guess," Anja said. "It's all crisis, crisis, crisis. Nobody has money except for a few foreign tourists. But we've got each other and this beautiful place."

"Yeah, I know what you mean, in Lisbon it's horrible, there are more and more beggars on the streets," Antonia said, hoping that maybe they would talk about the dead girls when she mentioned Lisbon. But no, they weren't opening up, so she continued with the small talk.

Eventually, after a couple of hours and many generous refills of their beer glasses, Antonia decided to take action. She had come prepared.

"Hey girls, look what I brought from Lisbon," she said, dangling a bottle of Jaegermeister liquor in front of them.

She remembered the dark liquor was their favorite and how they had complained about not being able to get hold of it in the Portuguese countryside. She whisked out some small glasses and poured.

"Oh Antonia, you remembered, you're going to make our evening," Anja said as she grabbed a glass and knocked it back.

The fire roared in front of them, sending flames into the calm moon-lit night as the sea lapped the shore. Moriba was fired up, though, and beat out an electrifying African tune on his bongos. Some of them got up and danced to the mesmerizing rhythm. Antonia drank less but kept pouring Jaegermeister out of the rectangular bottle and mixing it with Red Bull, to make Jaegerbombs for the girls. Soon they were giggling and drunk. Antonia thought it's now or never.

"I was so sorry to hear about Brigitte and Katja," she said. "It must have been terrible for you."

"It is still unbelievable, surreal," Heike said. "I still think I will see them here at any moment. It was so mindless."

"But what actually happened?" Antonia said. "I just don't understand, why them?"

"I don't know, I'm a bit scared," Anja said. "I don't know what to say."

"What do you mean?" Antonia said. "If you're scared about anything, you should talk to the authorities. You can tell me, I used to be a cop, I'll keep it between us."

"Well, they were acting strangely before they left for Lisbon, really nervous," Anja said. "They tried to hide it but it was obvious. Something was going on."

"Did they say anything before they left?" Antonia said.

"They did, that's what's so worrying," Anja said, glancing at Heike.

"What was it?" Antonia said, knowing she had to keep pushing the point now.

"They didn't talk a lot in the days before they left, but they said a few things," Anja said. "They talked about some kind of a plan, an evil plan."

"Was that it?" Antonia said.

"They mentioned a woman in Germany, in Frankfurt, who knew something about it. Then I overheard them say something like 'Lisbon water kills'," Anja said. "It didn't make sense, but it sounded scary."

"What should we do Antonia?" Heike asked.

"I don't think you should do anything, just be quiet about it, don't tell anybody else," Antonia said.

Antonia felt a pang of guilt at how she got the information she needed but ultimately what she was doing was trying to find justice for Brigitte and Katya. She sipped some more Jaegermeister and looked at Dieter, who was strumming Bob Dylan's 'Like a Rolling Stone' on his guitar in between puffs on a joint.

She left the girls, who were giggling from the drink and gave her a knowing look as she sauntered over to Dieter. She kissed him on the cheek as she sat down on the log next to him.

"Hi darling, how are you?" she whispered in his ear.

"Oh, I'm just swell," he said, smiling and happy from drink and dope.

"Maybe we should think about going back to your tepee," she said, having forgotten all about Miguel back in the hostel.

He laughed a little. "Just let me finish this song."

"Okay, but don't take too long."

Eventually, he put the guitar down and she looked into his eyes, smiling. She slipped her arm around him and led him back to the path from the beach.

She loved the inside of his tepee, with its tatami floor, handicrafts and ornaments, the rocking chair with books stacked alongside it and the generous futon bed draped with fluffy blankets.

"Do you want a drink, a joint?" he said.

"Why don't you roll us a great, big joint, my lover," she said, pulling him towards the bed. She loved it when he got high, he was like a child.

He sat cross-legged and got the tobacco out while she rested her head in his lap, tickling the inside of his thighs. He finished rolling the joint, lit up and had a puff as she started to unbutton his shirt and stretched her hands up his chest. Then he reached inside her jumper and caressed her breasts. He pulled off her jumper and pinched her nipples gently before moving in to take them in his mouth.

She sat up and kissed his lean torso. Then she undressed completely and whispered gently in his ear to do the same. He remained sitting and she eased her curvaceous body down on him as he grabbed her buttocks, lifting her gently up and down with his strong arms. They kissed as she leaned forward, rubbing her breasts against him.

As they finished, Dieter lay down and smoked the joint, occasionally offering her some. She took it but didn't inhale as she drew on it. He played with her hair and her breasts as they lay there. He dozed off.

Antonia rolled out of the bed and quietly pulled her clothes back on. As she snuck out of Dieter's tepee, she thought what a beautiful, lovely man he was. She had adored the few times she had been with him. It had taken her mind off things. But the two of them could never be a couple – he was just too laid back for her, she knew it would get on her nerves eventually. But she also knew he was there whenever she came back, and he wouldn't demand anything from her.

Under the moonlight, she walked carefully around his tepee to Brigitte and Katya's tent and unzipped the entrance flap. Inside was just as she remembered it, nobody had touched anything. She turned on a flashlight and looked through the little bookshelf and table with their personal belongings next to their bed. She looked for little nooks where they might have hidden things, but found nothing. She picked up books and flipped through them. She was about to give up and go when a slip of paper dropped out of a history book she was holding.

"Helga – Frankfurt," it read, followed by a telephone number and an email address. It must be the woman in Germany who Anja talked about. Antonia tucked it into her back pocket and walked along the dunes to the hostel.

Miguel had gone to bed early but that hadn't stopped him from worrying about Antonia. He was irritated when she came down to breakfast.

"So, where were you all night?" he said. "You sure took your time."

He had heard her returning to her room at four in the morning.

"It just took that much time, I had to get them in the mood to talk," she said. "But I think I got a good lead."

She told Miguel about everything – the contact in Frankfurt and them saying "Lisbon water kills." She didn't want him to feel that she was holding anything back in the hope that he wouldn't pursue her friends any further. Of course, she didn't tell him about Dieter. He listened and nodded.

"Do you think they know anything else?" Miguel said.

"I really don't think so, I don't believe they would keep things from me," she said. "We've got to follow up this Frankfurt lead."

He seemed satisfied and agreed to leave it at that. If need be they could return with a warrant, he thought.

They checked out of the hostel and began walking to the car when they spotted a big Mercedes with diplomatic plates drive past and stop outside a cafe. They kept their distance and saw Wolfgang step out of the car. Antonia was incensed. He was intruding on her peaceful idyll.

"What the blue fuck are you doing here?" she said as she strode up to him.

"I am on official business," Wolfgang said. He turned to Miguel. "Hi Miguel."

"Hi Wolfgang," Miguel said as Antonia glared at the unwelcome visitor.

Wolfgang turned his back on them and went inside the cafe.

"Look, he's allowed to go where he wants in Portugal," Miguel said to Antonia. "I can't stop him. It's a free country," he said. "But maybe this time we shouldn't give him any help."

"Well, he doesn't seem to need any, does he?" she said with sarcasm in her voice.

"Okay, I agree, let's just leave him and head back to Lisbon," he said as they walked to the car.

*

Lying in her hospital bed, Antonia reflected that they could have killed her, gotten her out of the way permanently. But killing a cop would have drawn too much heat, probably brought in the FBI, and the small-time politicians in a small Massachusetts town wouldn't have been able to handle that. It was just a warning, though the asshole they got to do it had likely botched it, got nervous and fired from too far away, doing more damage than his bosses intended.

She gingerly tried to turn onto her side and felt a stab of pain that made her stop. She looked at the drips and sighed, told herself to be patient. She could be off her feet for six weeks, they said.

She'd had dozens of visitors since coming out of the operating theatre and recovering consciousness.

Almost all of them were family. In her fragile state, she was moved to tears by her parents' anguish. They had once encouraged her to join the force. Now they feared for their only child's life. "You're sticking your neck out, baby," her dad said to her quietly. "It's time to pull it back in."

Mike, her ex, had stopped by but said he was going on duty and couldn't stay long. No cops came to see her. She just got flowers from the police department.

Her superiors were explaining away the shooting as a result of rising crime as unemployment in the town soared with the collapse of the garment industry. And of course the public spending cuts left the police with little manpower to investigate a shooting with no witnesses.

She knew she wasn't popular for speaking out against the ruinous cocaine addiction gripping the town and afflicting the entire state. Too many of the users were well-connected middle-class types, and too many people were either embarrassed by it all or simply getting rich off it. She risked causing friction, like in the Cheryl Araujo gang rape case back in the bar of a nearby town in the 80s when she was a young teen. The Portuguese-American community had to circle the wagons then but she doubted they'd do the same for her now.

Being a cop had taught her to tone down her natural irreverence and control her short fuse. But that didn't mean she had to be anyone's stooge.

After some former high-school friends who were now heavily into coke gave her some tips about where the drug was coming from, she couldn't just ignore what was going on. But the District Attorney blocked a formal investigation after an initial – and feeble – inquiry. Going along with the scandalous decision stuck in her craw.

Unable to let the matter drop, she started asking questions in the Portuguese bars she frequented. Someone must have overheard her or tipped off her superiors – probably Frank Guedes, the local gossip with his wife Josefa.

She was asking for trouble, Antonia knew that. But she couldn't help herself. It was like when she went into the rough surf in Caparica as a child and almost drowned.

"You have to be true to yourself," she whispered to herself in her hospital bed.

Once she recovered, the department unceremoniously pushed her out. She tried to push back, but her chief told her she was regarded as no longer fit for duty and, when she tried to argue, went to the heart of it.

"Some people upstairs aren't happy," he said. "They say you've gone rogue."

"I was just doing my job," she said.

"You're a beat cop, not a detective. Knowing your place is a virtue around here."

She was pensioned off and given a lump sum in compensation for her injury. She could have fought the decision in the courts, but she didn't have the money for drawn-out litigation.

She had had it coming. She had been naïve. She was just as angry at herself as at them. But the episode that changed the course of her life left a sour taste of betrayal and a deep feeling of contempt. To help put it behind her, she used the money to move back to Portugal.

They'd stopped her that time. But it wouldn't happen again.

Chapter 7

Miguel left home in a foul mood. He got in his car, aggressively revved it and pulled abruptly out into the Lisbon traffic, bringing shouted curses and fist-shaking from the builders' van he cut up. Another bitter argument with his wife was a nasty start to the day. Fuming, he tried to switch his thoughts to his job – and Antonia, who he was going to pick up. He had the warrant to search Brigitte and Katja's apartment in his pocket.

Miguel drove across the city to the Alfama district, maneuvering his unmarked police car through the narrow, hilly streets, and biting his lip as he got stuck behind the picturesque yellow trams that trundled through the old part of town. He couldn't let his superiors find out he was taking Antonia along on the search, but he didn't mind relaxing the rules a bit. He wasn't an uptight person. And Antonia had a lot of inside knowledge to offer the investigation. Truth be told, he looked forward to seeing her, especially as the atmosphere at home had become so suffocating.

Anyway, Wolfgang wasn't an official either and Miguel had been instructed to liaise closely with him. Wolfgang's involvement was a political consideration, Miguel thought to himself, to keep Germany and its tourists happy. German holidaymakers always cited safety as a key concern when choosing their vacations, and hundreds of thousands of them came to Portugal each year. Miguel had little patience for the politics of his job, but he knew he ignored those interests at his peril.

Miguel had asked around the office about Wolfgang. Information on Herr Müller was not easy to come by, though. Miguel discovered that Wolfgang had been in a special unit of the Bundespolizei before moving to Lisbon a year or so ago. Miguel suspected Wolfgang had friends in high places to get such a cushy embassy posting.

Wolfgang had started his career in Munich in the 1970s, with that city's private security force nicknamed by locals the *schwarze Sheriffs* – not just because of their all-black uniforms and the mirror sunglasses they commonly wore, which made them look intimidating, like modern-day stormtroopers, but also because they at times seemed to be a law unto themselves, and reputedly pretty brutal with it. Wolfgang was well-built, for sure, but didn't come across as threatening at all. He had been very helpful whenever Miguel had called him, and Miguel's superiors had shown no qualms about keeping Wolfgang in the loop.

As he approached St. George's Castle near where Antonia lived, Miguel felt an urge to get things off his chest with her, to come clean with her completely, to lay out his ideas, his dreamed-of plans for them, what they could do together. At the same time, he was worried she might think him a pest. His wife certainly wasn't keen on Antonia being around. She regarded Antonia as a threat. The struggle to make ends meet and his long working hours continued to cause friction between Miguel and his wife. His son, who was soon to turn nine, was increasingly moody and withdrawn and no longer wanted to go out and play football with his dad. That pained Miguel deeply. He felt like he'd been dealt a bad hand by life.

Middle-age seemed to have clouded things instead of clarifying them, as Miguel had expected. He wasn't sure any more whether his wife was having an affair or whether he was just being overly suspicious – or even if he was imagining it to give himself a way out of his marriage. What a mess. He didn't want to dump all that on Antonia. She had made it clear the last time he broached the subject that it was his problem to deal with. His heart told him, though, that Antonia had to be his break with the recent past – and the making of a better future. It looked like he'd come to a watershed in his life. And he had to get Antonia before someone else snapped her up – a pretty, sassy woman like her wouldn't stay alone for long. And she was obviously at a loose end herself after leaving America.

Antonia climbed into the car. "*Bom dia,*" she said, searching Miguel's expression for a clue to his mood.

"How's it going?" he said, setting off without delay.

Antonia wound down the window and lit a cigarette. She sensed Miguel was irritable but she didn't have the patience right then to question him about it. She was in a pensive frame of mind, her thoughts repeatedly wandering back to the carefree atmosphere of Aljezur. Antonia knew she had to get to the bottom of what had happened to Brigitte and Katja before she would be able to focus her mind on other things.

The drive over to Rolf's building wasn't easy. The downtown traffic diversions had caused virtual gridlock. People, peeved by their falling standard of living and their feeling of powerlessness, took their frustration out on other drivers. The fierce hooting in the long traffic jams was at times a cacophony, echoing off the buildings and forcing pedestrians to cover their ears.

Miguel joined in the shouting but Antonia sat back and tried to relax in the warm autumn sunshine coming through the windows. The downpour had been something of a freak event as the Indian summer, known to locals as St. Martin's summer, continued. Unknown to Antonia and Miguel, they passed close by the office where Mario was desperately trying to conjure up some workable – and affordable – solution for the Baixa.

"Are you going to Aunt Fatima's lunch on Sunday?" Miguel asked, making an effort to be sociable and break the silence.

"Yes," Antonia said. "Are you and your wife going?"

Miguel shifted uneasily in his seat, then banged on the car hooter in frustration. They fell back into silence.

When they got to Rolf's building, Wolfgang was waiting outside for them. Antonia gave Miguel a withering look as they parked. He shrugged and got out.

Antonia pointedly ignored Wolfgang. Miguel shook hands with him and they exchanged pleasantries.

"Well, we know the front door's open," Miguel said. "Which is just as well, because I haven't got the key." He pushed open the door for Antonia, then Wolfgang ushered him in. They went straight up to the 4th floor, Antonia trotting ahead.

Outside Brigitte and Katja's apartment, Miguel pulled rubber gloves out of his pocket and gave some to Antonia and Wolfgang. He turned the key in the lock and opened the door.

Miguel and Antonia gasped. Their jaws dropped at the scene of destruction in front of them. The apartment had been completely trashed. They stepped inside and cast their eyes over the damage – the slashed-open cushions, sofa and mattress, the broken lamps and paintings. They stepped gingerly through the wreckage as they went through the rooms. The fridge was overturned, cupboards torn off the walls, crockery smashed. The only sound was a ticking clock that had escaped the onslaught.

"It looks like a tornado came through here," Antonia said. She felt a chill – the devastation reminded her of how violence had suddenly intruded in her peaceful friends' lives.

"It appears someone was looking for something and got very angry when they couldn't find it," Miguel said.

"We have to check whether the neighbors heard anything," Antonia said.

"The other apartments are all empty," Wolfgang said. "I checked."

Antonia and Miguel waded into the mess. Wolfgang didn't show much interest. He leaned on the door jamb and watched them work. Miguel appreciated Wolfgang diplomatically keeping his distance. But Antonia thought, what a slacker – he probably thinks this kind of stuff is beneath him. She didn't say anything, though. Miguel had asked her to keep the peace, and she had given him her word. She didn't want to make life hard for him, though she didn't know how she could make it any sweeter. She was fond of him, always had been. But he was married, however tenuously, and Antonia insisted on honesty and frankness.

Miguel began taking photographs of the scene. Wolfgang stepped back into the stairwell, keeping out of the pictures.

In the bedroom, clothes were torn to shreds and strewn around. Antonia knelt down and picked through the books scattered around the floor. There was a Time Out guide to Lisbon, a well-thumbed copy of Barry Hatton's "The Portuguese: A Modern History," a collection of Fernando Pessoa's poetry in English – all normal stuff you'd expect to find on the bookshelves of a foreigner's apartment in Lisbon. There was also a slim volume of Tagus tidal information and a coffee-table history book about the rebuilding of the downtown district after the 1755 earthquake. Antonia frowned. That's a bit nerdy for Brigitte and Katja, she thought. She figured they must be Rolf's and set them aside. There wasn't much else to look at.

"Did they travel light?" Miguel asked Antonia.

"They lived light," she said. "They weren't the type to collect modern baubles like iPhones and iPads and stuff. Their ambition was to keep life simple and honest, uncluttered. Not that they were against modern technology, or anything. They used email and the Internet."

"Well, they'd only been here a few days and presumably they weren't intending a long stay," Miguel said. "It's probably been picked clean. It seems we're running behind the curve on this investigation."

Antonia stood a chair back up against a wall, beneath a bedroom window which had a spectacular view over Lisbon. "They could never have afforded to stay in an apartment as nice as this," she said, turning to Miguel.

"What is he saying, this Rolf person?" asked Wolfgang, who was now at the bedroom door.

"He's clammed up," Miguel said. "He told us they'd paid him rent, but not how much. Though I think we can guess why he may have given it to them cheaply."

Antonia shivered. "A first-class degenerate. Makes my skin crawl. But a psychopath?"

"Forensics found a strand of the murdered French woman's hair in Rolf's apartment," Miguel said, checking in his notebook. "Wolfgang reckons if we keep looking we'll find Brigitte and Katja's, too. Rolf's fingerprints were in the French woman's apartment. But it's all plausible. We haven't got enough to charge him at the moment. And we'll have to let him go soon."

"Even with all the sordid voyeur stuff?" Antonia said.

"It depends on how solid we can make our case. We need to identify and find the other ones he filmed," Miguel said. "And he's rich so he has smart lawyers. But we should be able to take his passport off him."

Amid the desolation and her friends' shredded clothes, Antonia felt an urge to break down in tears; and she was growing increasingly irritated by Wolfgang just skulking there by the door, doing nothing. She pretended to find something under the duvet.

"Oh look," she said, "here's their cellphone!"

Wolfgang darted over. Antonia turned to him and, with a big grin, said, "Just kidding."

Miguel tried to look annoyed with her but he couldn't help smiling. Wolfgang had a face like thunder. "We are not making jokes," he said through gritted teeth.

Miguel tried to defuse the tension. "Let's see how he got the photos and videos," he said, looking around at the walls and ceiling. "And let's start there," he said, pointing at a smoke detector above their heads.

They pulled up chairs and Miguel and Wolfgang got knives from the kitchen. They poked at the detector till it came away from the plaster – followed by a fiber-optic camera.

"Bingo!" Miguel said.

"Scumbag," Antonia said.

"I'll call in the techies. There must be more of these things around," Miguel said. "Let's see if we can pin it to Rolf."

*

Two dozen reporters, photographers and a bank of television cameras waited expectantly in a Lisbon hotel's conference room for the entrance of Chantal LeBlanc's parents. The press conference by the murdered French woman's mother and father was scheduled for 8 p.m., at the start of Portuguese television's evening news programs, and the three main channels planned to go live.

An exclusive interview the parents had given to a major Lisbon newspaper had appeared that day, and it pulled no punches in its criticisms of the Portuguese authorities. Now it was the turn of the rest of the media pack to twist the knife into a government that had done itself no favors with its frequently high-handed, distant attitude towards the press.

The reporters got what they wanted, in spades. While his wife choked back tears in her dignified grief, Monsieur LeBlanc's finger-wagging outburst of Gallic ire went straight to the heart of the government's weak handling of crises since it came to power. Jean LeBlanc demanded to know why no progress had been made in finding his daughter's murderer, why her parents were being kept in the dark, and why no new security measures had been put in place in tourist areas. "After two weeks...*quinze jours*...nothing, *rien*," he shouted. "I will tell the people of France to avoid Lisbon. I will say, Do not go to Lisbon. It is a place...*dangereux*!"

The press lapped it up. Hoteliers, bar and restaurant owners and shopkeepers were alarmed.

Portuguese officials, called in to react to the Frenchman's accusations, squirmed. Portugal's judicial secrecy law, which prohibited the release of information pertaining to an ongoing police investigation, gagged them, they said.

But the next day, a judiciously leaked story earned broad coverage. A front-page article in *Jornal do Dia* ran under the headline, "Women tourist killings: Swiss millionaire arrested." It flew in the face of the judicial secrecy law, but no officials complained – everyone knew that the law was a sham anyway. "Police investigating the deaths of three women tourists in Lisbon have arrested a Swiss millionaire," the story said. It included a police mug shot of Rolf and a photo of his Lisbon apartment building.

"Rolf Fankhauser, 36, was detained earlier this week at one of the Lisbon buildings he owns," the report said. "Fankhauser is a former hippy who used to live in a commune in Aljezur. The encampment is known for drug use and free love. The wiry, blonde-haired Swiss turned his back on the hippy life after he inherited a family fortune last year. Police sources tell *Jornal do Dia* that he is also suspected of involvement in Internet porn."

The murders had further unsettled a government already on the ropes over the bailout and austerity policies and now reeling from the calamity in the Baixa, which was swiftly turning into a political disaster and a public relations catastrophe. The authorities came across as lame and clueless. Polls put the beleaguered government's popularity at around 20 percent – a record low. People were taking bets on how long the government would last. Some of the ruling party's apparatchiks were already devoting time and effort to ensuring their post-government well-being. There was, rumor had it, some shameless nest-feathering going on.

Successfully solving the murders would make the government look good and bring it some respite, however briefly. With the secretary of state for home affairs demanding results, senior police detectives recommend that Miguel be placed in charge of the investigation. He was, they said, diligent, discreet and diplomatic – and unlikely to cause any more headaches for the politicians.

Miguel was at first reluctant to take the job on. It would mean more work, more pressure, more time away from home. He complained that he wouldn't get any more pay, either, but his superiors assured him it was a quick way to earn a promotion, as long as he solved the case and didn't screw up.

Miguel relented. Before calling his wife with the news, he called Antonia on her cellphone.

"Listen, there's been a change," he said. "I've been moved upstairs, given extra responsibilities, and I won't be able to bring you along like before."

"I see," Antonia said, "congratulations." She felt a twinge of rejection that she tried to ignore. "I presume you'll still be holding Wolfgang's hand, though."

Miguel decided to ignore that. "I'm in charge of the tourist killer case. It's a big opportunity for me."

Antonia rolled her eyes. "You're being set up as a patsy! You'll end up taking the fall, can't you see that?"

"I deserve the recognition, I think. I've worked hard for this," Miguel said indignantly.

"It's ridiculous! The police are going down the wrong track, just because of pressure from the newspapers," Antonia said. "It's like the tail's wagging the dog."

"And you've got it all worked out, have you?"

"They're separate cases," Antonia said. "The only thing the murders have in common was that the victims were staying at the same apartment and that they were foreigners. It's circumstantial. I told you what Brigitte and Katja had told me in Aljezur, that they were on to something big up here. And Heike and Anja confirmed that. And there's the Frankfurt connection and…"

"You're jumping to conclusions," Miguel said. "You can't make your mind up about what happened until we've dug around properly. I know they were friends of yours but how well did you really know them? They could have been some of those crazy conspiracy theorists who spend too much time in their wigwam getting stoned, having free love and surfing the web."

Antonia, at the other end of the phone, seethed at that, and her anger rendered her speechless. "And anyway," Miguel said, "everything points in one direction at the moment, and Rolf is the common denominator."

"Rolf! That wacko?" Antonia said. "He's just a freak! And he couldn't punch his way out of a wet paper bag, much less kill anyone."

"Well that may be," Miguel said, relishing how he was going to break the latest news from his investigation team. "But how do you explain this: there was a kilo of coke under his sink, inside a box of washing powder."

Antonia was about to say something but Miguel kept going. "And some of the 'candid' photos on his computer bear a striking resemblance to Chantal LeBlanc," Miguel said triumphantly.

"Oh bullshit," Antonia shouted. "I've told you before. We need to track down this woman Helga in Frankfurt."

Miguel's frustration boiled over. He knew he was taking it out on his dear Antonia, but he couldn't stop himself. "Look, I'm not a 'free spirit' like you," he shouted. "I've got a job to do. I need my pay check at the end of the month. Don't forget I've got a house and a-…" he stopped himself.

"That's right," Antonia said pointedly. "See you all Sunday at Aunt Fatima's." She hung up.

Antonia sighed and tried to compose herself. She'd thought moving back to Portugal would be quiet and restful. Fat chance. Life was full of surprises.

She went into the kitchen and poured herself a glass of wine. She lit a cigarette and went out onto the balcony to look at the bright lights in the riverside square where the workmen seemed to be standing around scratching their heads.

Antonia went back inside, changed into her pajamas and put her hair up into a bun. She picked up her file on the murders and scattered the cuttings over the floor. She put a Bob Marley album on and sat sipping her wine, looking at the bits of paper and photographs. It did look like just one case, she admitted to herself, but something just wasn't right and she couldn't ignore it.

She wished she had a whiteboard she could put up and work on. "Screw it," she said and started tacking everything to the bare white wall. She would get it repaired later so her aunt and uncle would never know.

She stuck up everything she had: photos of Brigitte and Katja, of Chantal LeBlanc and of Rolf. She added a magazine picture of the Elevador de Santa Justa and the Baixa. She wrote "Frankfurt/Helga" and "Aljezur" in pencil. As an afterthought, she wrote "Tagus tides" on one side with a question mark. Along the top, she wrote: "Lisbon water kills."

Antonia stood back and sipped her wine, nodding her head in time to the reggae beat. She was on her own with this now. She would have to stay focused and determined. She owed it to Brigitte and Katja. After a while she went over to the wall and tapped her pencil on "Frankfurt/Helga." She pulled out of the file the piece of paper with Helga's contacts, picked up her cellphone and punched in the number. The phone was turned off, and Antonia got a message in German she couldn't understand, so she hung up. She turned on her iPad and started composing an email to Helga.

"Deutschland, here I come," she said.

Chapter 8

Mario's new responsibilities were beginning to take their strain on him. He was reminded every morning of the growing challenges of his task as he passed through the downtown district on his way to work. It was a mess – silt and rubble from collapsed masonry filled Commercial Square. Noisy digging machines and trucks rolled across the grey square to clear the rubble, choking the air with black fumes. Engineers sat under tarpaulins that acted as their temporary offices, scouring architectural and structural charts of buildings and overseeing the clean-up operation.

As Mario arrived at his office in the public works ministry and sat down at his oak desk, Margarida greeted him with a cup of coffee and looked warily at the dark rings under his eyes.

"You have to look after yourself, I hope you're getting enough sleep boss," she said.

"I know, Margarida, I know," he said. "I just didn't imagine how much worry this would involve."

"Have you seen the papers this morning?" she said, knowing there was no way to protect him from the news.

He sifted through the headlines of the newspapers that Margarida neatly put on the side of his desk every morning, the financial ones that he preferred stacked on top.

"Finance ministry hit by disaster, computers out of action," read one headline. "Finance ministry out of batteries, civil servants lost in dark!," read another, followed by an article describing every detail of the damage at the ministry and the possibility of an evacuation of all government buildings downtown. It cited sources at the public works ministry.

Mario lowered his head into his hands and muttered 'dammit' to himself as he thought about what to do next. But Margarida beat him to it.

"You are supposed to meet the engineers at 10, you might want to get going," she said. "Leave the phone calls to me, I'll keep them at bay."

The phone started to ring the moment Margarida stopped talking but he gestured to her not to pick it up. He knew the deputy prime minister would be fuming. But he also knew that his best defense against accusations of wrongdoing was to be as professional as possible, and right now his most urgent task was to get the facts right about the damage on the ground himself. All else could wait.

"You're a gem Margarida," he said as he ran out. "Thanks for buying me some time."

Journalists were huddled at the ministry's front door so he instructed his driver to leave by the back entrance. Mario wrapped his jacket tight and looked up at the brisk, gun-metal sky overhead as they sped towards Commercial Square.

The driver drove into the square and was waved through the roadblocks that had been erected everywhere to cordon off the area. Mario stepped out of the car and looked over to the dark blue waters of the Tagus River. Centuries ago, this was just a sandy beach and the river's waters would creep into the city at high tide. During the Age of Expansion, ships offloaded their exotic wares on the quay here – spices, jewels and cloth – from far-flung corners of the world. In a sense it had been the epicenter of the riches from Portugal's global empire. The Marquis of Pombal renamed it Praca do Comercio – Commercial Square.

Mario walked over to the central tent on the square, past generators that were still pumping water from surrounding buildings with flooded basements. It was the second time he had visited the disaster area for a first-hand report of the damage. The first time, a couple of days after the disaster, there had been just too much chaos to draw any conclusions. That was days ago.

Professor Carla Gomes stood up when Mario approached, stepping back from the plastic table that was covered with charts and rulers and other instruments used to gauge the scale of the water damage to buildings and transport infrastructure in the area.

"Morning, Mr. Goncalves," she said, stretching out her hand through the thick sleeves of her heavy jacket. "As you can see, it's just a small disaster."

One of Portugal's foremost structural engineering experts, Carla was known for her dry humor. She usually spent her time in disaster hot spots, like Haiti after its earthquake, advising the United Nations on urban structural damage as a consultant. The Lisbon disaster meant she was working in her native Portugal for once. She had agreed to forego her exorbitant fees which broke Portugal could hardly afford, meaning she exercised her scathing directness with full force in her reports, having no paymaster to suck up to but only a sense of duty to help with the disaster that had hit her home country.

"Morning professor," said Mario, who had specifically sought out Carla for his disaster team. "What cheerful news do you have for me today?!"

She smiled, her long, jet black hair falling around her shoulders under the yellow hard hat she wore on her head.

"Well, I just don't get it, how it got this bad," she said. "The men are saying this was an act of God."

Mario pondered her words and remembered that the 1755 earthquake, which was Portugal's biggest natural disaster, was described in the same way. The 1755 disaster resulted in the reconstruction of Lisbon's entire downtown area, giving it that distinctive, grandiose flair that Mario so adored.

"Surely, we've moved on from that sort of thing, this disaster can be explained, can't it?" said Mario, huddling in the cold next to Carla, the group of engineers and local council experts she worked with.

"Yes, of course it can be explained, but the cock-ups that have made the damage so bad, can't be," she said.

"What do you mean?" said Mario.

"Somebody should have prepared for the possibility of this happening, that's all," she said. "After all, this is not 1755."

"Okay, fine, but can we just focus on the facts for now," said Mario. "I need to know how bad it is now, what your evaluation is and what we need to do about it."

Carla was well versed in talking to government officials and politicians and she knew that the only way to make them understand things was to show them. So she handed Mario a hard hat, called a couple of other engineers to join them, and started their tour of what they referred to as the 'disaster zone.'

As they began to walk, Carla pulled out of her jacket pocket a notebook where she had jotted down everything about the disaster. They walked across the square, towards the grand arch leading into the pedestrian street of Rua Augusta that stretched like a long finger from the square into town.

Apart from the heaving machines humming on the square, it was deadly quiet – the cafes around the square were all shut, the bustle of tourists walking around was gone and none of the picturesque yellow trams that give Lisbon a special charming touch were running in that part of town.

"To the virtues of our ancestors, who taught us all we know," read the inscription on top of the arch as they approached the edge of the square. Mario pondered the words etched into the stone and thought the country had all but forgotten them, not least the hard-working spirit of adventure that had given Portugal its proud past. Now, the nation was bust and had been forced to go cap in hand to the European Union and IMF. Perhaps the destruction on the square was a wake-up call, he thought.

Carla led them up the street under the arch and stopped. Shuttered shop windows lined the street, the outside tables and chairs used by the normally bustling restaurants were scattered everywhere, and sand and grit covered the pavement. A dark sludge and rubbish covered the street.

"So, that's just what you can see," said Carla. "What you can't see is how many of these buildings still have flooded or waterlogged basements."

"So, how many?" said Mario.

"Well, it stretches up at least three blocks," said Carla. "And you can draw a half circle from that point down to the river, so we're talking about a big chunk of real estate. It easily covers all the ministries down here."

"So, how long would it take to just clean up the shops and restaurants in the area, to get commerce up and running?" said Mario.

"Maybe a few months," said Carla. "But the problem is we don't have enough heavy machinery. The machines and pumps we have are now all dedicated to cleaning up the ministries."

"Okay, I guess we should head to the ministries then," said Mario.

They turned down one of the side streets as the sky turned darker and it started to rain in a reminder of that fateful night a few weeks before. It also demonstrated how difficult the clean-up operation had been as the unusually wet autumn made it hard to dry out the buildings.

Several thick hoses extended out of the central bank building, stretched tight as water pumped through them from the basement. Inside was a mess – there were piles of furniture scattered about and the reinforced glass doors that visitors usually passed through to enter were shattered on the marble floor.

Three guards standing at the entrance smiled at Carla and led them into the foyer.

"Quite a mess," Mario said to the guards.

"Yeah, and the clean up sure is taking its time, you can barely notice any progress," said one of them.

"Can we have a look at the basement?" Mario asked Carla.

"Sure, it's this way," she said, leading the group across the foyer to a corridor with a staircase at the end.

Mario followed close behind her as they slowly descended the stairs towards semi-darkness. Carla pulled out a torch from her pocket and lit up their downward path.

"So, no electricity at all then, I take it?" said Mario.

"Nowhere, not for many blocks," said Carla. "Apart from a few mobile generators we're using to bring some power to the ministries."

A stench met them as they approached the bottom of the stairs. Then they saw black, sludgy water lapping against the walls and stairs, about half a meter high. Through the semi-darkness that was interspersed with beams of light from torches, Mario could discern several forms standing deep in the water – men working to fix electric fittings and attempting to find ways to get the water out through the blocked drains.

"Can you call one of them over so I can talk to them?" he said to Carla.

"Sure, I'll call the foreman over," she said, then called out the name Pedro through the darkness.

A man waded through the water, sending small waves towards Mario and Carla, who huddled on the stairs just above the water line.

"Hi, how's it going professor?" said Pedro, stopping by the first underwater step and stretching out his arm to shake Carla's hand. He wore special boots that reached his waist.

"All good, thanks," said Carla, pointing to Mario. "This gent is from the public works ministry and has a few questions about your work, if you don't mind."

"No worries. Shoot," Pedro said, looking up at Mario.

"So, how bad is all this?" said Mario. "Is there anything working here?"

"No, nothing at all works," said Pedro. "And frankly I struggle to understand how we are going to get all this working again, even if we had all the equipment we need."

"Why is that?" said Mario.

"Because, apart from all the electrical systems being kaput, the drainage systems were overwhelmed by the storm," said Pedro. "Basically, the floodwaters mixed with sewage and it's all still down here. That's dangerous, a health risk, we can't get in to fetch things, it's all slippery and black with sewage."

"Damn!" said Mario. "In other words, it's too dirty to fix."

"That more or less sums it up," said Pedro.

Mario thanked Pedro for his time and turned to Carla, who's I-told-you-so look was becoming more conspicuous by the minute.

"I'm getting the picture," he told her as they turned to go back up the stairs.

"And this is not the worst," she said. "Wait till you see the finance ministry."

The central bank was a relatively small building and due to security requirements its walls and structure had been reinforced in recent years. That wasn't the case at the ministries.

They left the building and walked back out into the rain, turning left towards the distinctive dark yellow finance ministry. The rain drove into the finance ministry building as they approached from the square along the main road, which was all that separated it from the river. Mario could easily imagine the river spilling over its bank 50 meters away and pouring straight into the ministry.

They entered through the big side entrance leading into a large courtyard which was now full of heavy machinery and generators. Electric cables ran into the building.

A senior ministry official called Sergio, who was Mario's main contact, came out to greet them.

"There's pandemonium here today with those headlines," he said.

"I can imagine," said Mario as they entered the large corridor running down the middle of the three-story building on the ground floor.

Water marks were clearly visible along the corridor walls and the place stank of humidity. Mario could see a few people at their desks, huddling up to portable electric heaters. Otherwise, it was quiet and clearly most staff were not coming into work.

"There's nothing here to cheer about," said Sergio. "As you know, the computers in the basement have been destroyed and we are only running on back-up generators."

"Yes, I know about all of that," said Mario. "What about the rest – the building's structure, how is that?"

"That's what I want to show you," said Sergio, leading them into a corner office.

He grabbed Mario's arm and pointed to a crack in the wall.

"We've also got bulging walls and masonry pushed out of line," said Sergio. "And that's not the only crack we've found. They may be small but they are dangerous and they are creeping up the building from the basement."

"Dangerous in what way?" said Mario, turning to one of the engineers in their group.

"Well, the fact that there are cracks here on the ground floor means there are probably cracks in the foundations of the building as well," said the engineer. "Once the building settles, we're extremely concerned we'll find subsidence and tilting. It's not just possible, it's likely."

"Subsidence and tilting? Oh God," said Mario, breathing heavily, looking at Carla.

Carla didn't smile this time and had basically let the facts speak for themselves so that Mario could draw his own conclusion, which was obvious – they had to evacuate the area.

"I didn't want to tell you at first, but it's been obvious for some time," she said. "The politicians just don't want to face the facts but there is nothing that can be done until all of this dries out, which could take months. In the meantime it's just too dangerous for anybody to work here."

Mario let it all sink in as they walked through the dim, grey corridor, where he could make out patches of humidity and paint peeling off the walls. It made him think of a sinking ship and wondered if there was any money to salvage it.

Chapter 9

Antonia rode the S-Bahn from the airport into the center of Frankfurt. Sitting in a window seat, she was captivated by the view. It was her first trip in Europe outside of Portugal.

First, the train traveled through thick pine forest, then dived into the tidy suburbs before the city's skyscrapers, standing like potent symbols of financial muscle, came into view, just before the light railway dipped underground. Looking at those tall monuments to the power of money, she thought of what Dieter and Brigitte and Katja had told her in Aljezur about why they fled to a small, mostly overlooked – and financially frail and vulnerable – corner of the continent. Germany was Europe's economic powerhouse, and there were no signs of austerity around here. Just prim, almost smug, material comfort. Antonia marveled at how the European Union, supposedly an assembly of equals, could contain such contrasts.

Antonia was also struck by the relative newness of what she saw. It was more like the United States than Portugal. All the buildings appeared to be postwar – which, she thought to herself, they must be. Frankfurt wasn't short of history, of course, as the guidebook had pointed out. It was the birthplace of the famous writer Goethe. Antonia had never read anything by Goethe. In fact, she couldn't even name one of his books. Schooling hadn't been her thing, and she doubted Goethe was ever on the Massachusetts syllabus anyway. Still, she figured her intuition and determination were her strong points, not her school grades.

Antonia had only a small cabin bag with her, seeing as she planned to stay only two nights. She hadn't reckoned, though, with the crowds. Frankfurt airport was the third busiest in Europe and, she should have known, never quiet. The other, anonymous passengers and their piles of baggage hemmed her into her seat and bore down on her.

She got out at the stop for Sachsenhausen, pulling her jacket tighter against the chilly afternoon. She always made the mistake of packing for the weather she had at home, and Lisbon was considerably warmer than Frankfurt, as well as sunnier. Antonia had booked a room at a small, cheap hotel in this part of the city. She had been seduced by the guide books' tales of Sachsenhausen's old world charm, its higgledy-piggledy houses, its cafes and boulevards which she hoped would remind her of where she lived in Lisbon. Unlike Frankfurt city center, which had been mostly flattened by bombs during the war, much of this riverside area was centuries old. And, walking to her hotel, Antonia was pleasantly surprised by the cosmopolitan mix of nationalities in what was continental Europe's financial hub and home of the euro currency. The German language grated, though, with its guttural tones making it sound like someone clearing their throat. Musical it wasn't.

After sending Helga an email from Lisbon, Antonia had spoken to her on the phone two days later. Helga said she was calling from a public payphone. It was a very brief call. Antonia had hoped to chat to her about various things, to get a feel for her and for what her relationship was with Brigitte and Katja. Maybe Helga didn't even know they were dead, and Antonia had been rehearsing the best way to break the news to someone she didn't even know. But Helga gave her no chance. She was cagey, edgy and to the point, but willing to meet up. When Antonia told her she was flying over, Helga made a note of her arrival time and hotel. "Don't tell anyone you're coming," Helga said and abruptly hung up.

Antonia didn't even know what Helga looked like. She would just have to wait for Helga to contact her.

As Antonia, street map in hand and noisily dragging her travel case across the cobblestones, approached her hotel a plump young woman came up to her from the side. She grabbed Antonia's arm and gently but firmly steered her away from the hotel door, whispering conspiratorially, "*Komm mit, komm mit.*"

Antonia, though flustered, fought her natural reaction to shrug the woman off and allowed herself to be led. The woman had a very sweet, round face and was about 10 years younger than Antonia. She had a mullet haircut and big gypsy earrings and wore colorful, baggy clothes. She seemed ill-at-ease.

"It's me," the woman said, glancing around while holding Antonia's arm tightly. "Were you followed from the airport?"

"What?" Antonia said.

"I'm Helga. It's me. Are you being followed?"

"I don't know. I haven't checked," Antonia said, suddenly recalling the crowds at the airport and on the train. "Was I supposed to?"

"*Sicher ist sicher,*" Helga said, bringing her face close to Antonia's. "Better safe than sorry, as you say."

Helga led Antonia down towards the River Main. Antonia's mind raced. She looked at Helga, but Helga was too busy looking around for something. They turned left and right, and Antonia got the impression Helga was making sure they weren't being tailed.

"In here," Helga said, and they ducked into an old cottage-like building that inside was a cozy bar with dark wooden fittings and a low ceiling. There were few patrons at this time of day, and the two women slid into a cubicle with high backs.

"One moment," Helga said, getting back up again.

She's a bag of nerves, Antonia thought.

"I am going to the toilet," Helga said. "I will order."

Helga passed by the bar and asked the waiter for two glasses of *Apfelwein*, the local type of cider. Antonia sat back and tried to settle in and get her breath back. She pushed her bag under her seat and looked around. She thought about her email to Helga. Antonia had told Helga how and where she'd got her contact, dropping what she hoped were familiar names, and mentioned a bit about Aljezur. At the same time, she had tried to suggest she knew about something confidential, something only Brigitte and Katja and Helga knew, even though she didn't have a clue if there was any such thing. It was just a hunch. The way things were panning out, there really was something going on. She was dying to find out, but she had to go steady, especially with Helga in the state she was.

When Helga came back and sat down, Antonia raised her glass and said with a smile, "Well, cheers."

"*Prost*," Helga replied and took a big gulp.

"So how did you recognize me?" Antonia asked with a smile. "I'm curious."

"I Googled you," Helga said. "I saw your photo in the American paper from when you were shot."

"Ah, I see," Antonia said.

"You are okay now, yes?" Helga asked.

"Oh yes, all fine and repaired. Back to normal," Antonia said.

Helga glanced nervously around the room. That seemed a good moment for Antonia to move the conversation forward. She leaned across the table, closer to Helga.

"So why so secretive?" Antonia asked in a low voice.

"You must be very careful," Helga said, though she seemed desperate to talk. "I have fear that my home and my telephone are bugged. Maybe even with cameras."

Antonia's mind jumped back to the scene in Rolf's apartment in Lisbon. She gulped.

"I have moved out of my home. I am staying with friends. And I am thinking I'm being followed," Helga said, running a hand nervously through her hair and looking around. "I don't know if I'm going mad. They might be cops or private detectives. Who knows? It's an underworld, all dark, nobody knows what's really going on. Except them."

"Hey, calm down," Antonia said. "We're safe here, the two of us."

"But that is just it – we're not! Look at what goes on in the world. You cannot trust the governments or the corporations. It is all fixed up behind the scenes. I mean, look at your American dollar bill! The eye of God, the number thirteen, the owl – the freemasons! Just look it up on the Internet!"

"Yeah, well, I'm as skeptical about the Internet as I am about politicians," Antonia said.

Helga, as if reading Antonia's thoughts, said, "You probably think I'm paranoid. A crazy German woman."

"No, no, no, not at all," Antonia said, reaching across the table to put a reassuring hand on Helga's arm. "Something's going on, I know that. I just need you to slow down a moment. I only flew in a few hours ago. My head's spinning. Bear with me." She took a sip of her drink and indicated for Helga to do the same.

"Okay, I know, I am sorry," Helga said. "What can I tell you? I work at the University of Applied Sciences. I know Brigitte and Katja from our student times."

Oh shit, Antonia thought, she doesn't know.

"They dropped out," Helga went on, "But I finished the course, eventually. I was not as brave as they were. I could not just stand up and walk away, do something better with my life like them. I was afraid. And now I'm more afraid."

Antonia was staring at her glass, her mind running through what she might say about their dead friends.

"You were with them in Aljezur, right?" Helga said, and Antonia nodded.

"I've been living back in Lisbon recently, though," Antonia said.

"Well, any friend of theirs is a friend of mine."

Helga signaled for the waiter to bring more drinks. A middle-aged couple, looking like tourists with cameras slung over their shoulders, came into the bar. Helga watched them closely before turning back to Antonia.

"I don't know how much you know but I'll start from the beginning," Helga said. "My boyfriend, Juergen – he was working with me at the university – was sent to Berlin for six months to work on a big IT project. At a construction company. This was a few months ago. It is a big company, very powerful and influential. With lots of friends," Helga said, giving Antonia a meaningful look.

Antonia nodded knowingly, eager for Helga to keep going.

"He is like me. He knows there are a lot of powers we can't see in the open. Hidden powers. Our world is made into *Scheisse* by these people. They have schemes to make themselves even more rich. Money is everything to them."

Antonia cleared her throat and shifted in her seat, hoping to nudge Helga into sticking to the point.

"Juergen emailed me an attachment. I sent it to Brigitte and Katja because I knew they were in Portugal and might be able to help me figure out what it meant."

"What kind of dossier was it?"

"It was called *Unternehmen Lissabon Wasser*."

"Unter- what? What does that mean?"

"Operation Lisbon Water."

Antonia frowned. "And?"

Helga had a gulp of cider and kept her voice low. "Juergen became suspicious. He was a lowly IT worker, so his bosses didn't pay much attention to him. He was invisible to them. Just, how do you say, a worker bee?"

Antonia nodded.

"Well," Helga went on, "one day they, the bosses, were talking and their door was open and Juergen heard what they were saying. Juergen hated these people. They were in bed with the politicians, the nationalists, big media people, you name it. One big conspiracy waiting to happen. So they're talking and Juergen is listening. They start saying things like, 'Time for our revenge!' and 'Time to get some of our money back!' So Juergen took a look at their computers. A bit of hacking, you know. And what he found was Operation Lisbon Water. That's what they were talking about."

Helga sat back and took a sip. Antonia kept looking at her.

"That's it? That's all?" Antonia said. "Didn't he find anything else?"

Helga became sad. "Well, no," she said, looking at her drink. "I haven't heard from Juergen for more than a week. And I'm worried."

Helga's eyes became moist. Antonia, regretting her abruptness, stretched both arms across the table to hold and comfort her. Helga pulled herself together.

"I knew Brigitte and Katja were in Portugal," Helga said. "They loved it there. I sent them the file to see what they thought. They said they'd look into it but I never heard back. Do you know anything?"

Antonia took a deep breath. "Helga, I've got some horrible news."

Helga looked alarmed, and her skin went pale.

"They're both dead," Antonia said.

Before Antonia could continue, Helga shot to her feet, knocking over her glass. "Dead? It's my fault!" she screamed. "That dossier is deadly. You see why I was being so careful? My boyfriend! You can't stay, get out of here," she said to Antonia as she picked up her bag and, in tears, fled out of the door.

Antonia was in shock. Other people in the bar were looking at her. Then, Helga barged back in and strode over to Antonia. Tears streaming down her cheeks, she bent down and whispered quickly into Antonia's ear, "Meet me at the *Dom* tomorrow at midday," then she turned and walked out.

Antonia went over to the bar and paid in silence as the waiter and the other drinkers watched her. She went outside, lit a cigarette and found her way back to the hotel. Despite her skeptical nature, she couldn't help looking over her shoulder as she walked. When she got to the hotel, she went around the back and went in through the small garden. Only a cat watched her.

Chapter 10

Carla waited patiently in the restaurant, looking intently at the fish swimming around in their tank by the window. It made her think of the situation in Lisbon and how the politicians, like the fish, could only move around in a confined space until their fate became inevitable. The fish would be eaten and the politicians would eventually have to call an evacuation of the downtown area. It was all so obvious.

Mario turned up half an hour late after another long day at the office. He was tired and had tried for hours to talk to the minister about the options available to them. But he had failed – the minister was just too busy, no doubt trying to work out how to draw maximum advantage out of the whole situation, Mario thought.

"I was beginning to be afraid that you had stood me up," Carla said, smiling as he approached.

They kissed on the cheek.

"Sorry, busy as usual," he said. "Things just haven't stopped for me, I'm constantly inundated."

Mario was a little intimidated by cosmopolitan Carla, who jetted around the world to international conferences and disaster zones as an unmarried woman in her early forties. She was everything he wasn't, with his stable, married life, kids and a steady job at the ministry. He had invited her to dinner after their visit to the disaster zone, thinking it would be good to get more information in an informal setting.

"So, did I give you enough to think about the other day?" she asked, sipping a gin and tonic.

"You sure did," he said. "I suppose I had imagined some of what you showed me, but seeing it all like that made the whole thing very clear. My problem is I am still just a civil servant and I have to convince the politicians. You know what that's like, I imagine."

"I most certainly do, I spend my entire life doing just about nothing else," she said. "But I guess the convincing I do only relates to disasters, life or death situations, like this. I can't imagine you have dealt with anything like this before?"

"No, this is most certainly a first," he said as the waiter came to take their orders. "I could probably learn a thing or two from you."

"What you have to remember about politicians is that they only think about one thing – how they can look good themselves," she said. "If they make a decision, it's only about how they look."

"Yeah, I'm learning that like never before," said Mario.

The food arrived and Mario leaned over to pour the fine red wine into Carla's glass. He wondered for a moment what it would be like to see her tipsy and poured her glass full.

A few glasses later and Carla was bubbly, telling stories of her adventures in far flung disaster zones and her run-ins with self-important politicians. Mario was enjoying himself and decided to try to pry for more information.

"So, what other thoughts have you had about our disaster?" said Mario.

"Well, there was another strange thing that night," she said.

"What do you mean?" said Mario. "You're making me worried now."

"I didn't really want to mention this the other day, but it seems there was some kind of tremor on that night."

Mario's stomach fluttered – the last thing he needed was even more trouble.

"An earthquake?" he said.

"Look, maybe I shouldn't have told you," she said. "It just seems there was some kind of earth tremor, there are indications and signs. What we have seen so far are some strange cracks in underground structures, close to the river. They can't be explained by the water damage."

Mario recalled that small tremors were often felt in Portugal – they were usually caused by the same Atlantic Ocean fault line that set off Lisbon's 1755 disaster.

"Perhaps that explains the scale of the damage?" he said.

"I am a scientist and I can only go on the facts. I have seen similar things to this in other places before, which subsequently turned out to be the consequences of earthquakes. But I can't tell you yet that I have direct evidence of it. We need more information."

Mario didn't push it any further – she had clearly said everything she knew. They finished their coffees and he asked for the bill.

"Thanks so much Carla, I really appreciate everything you are doing," he said as they left the restaurant. "Please let me know as soon as you learn anything else about the tremor."

They said good-night and Mario walked through the cool autumn night towards his waiting car. He was agitated and jittery, not quite knowing how to handle this latest bit of information from Carla. It was strange and unnerving that a tremor should coincide with the torrential rain and high tide on that fateful night, he thought.

*

Mario slept badly and grew increasingly determined to talk to his boss the following morning. But when he arrived at work, he was told that the minister had decided to go on a skiing trip to the Swiss Alps early in the season. How the hell could he leave at this time for a long weekend, Mario thought to himself.

At the same time that Mario arrived at the ministry, his boss Jorge Fontana slipped into his first-class seat on a flight bound for Geneva with work the last thing on his mind. Jorge dozed off at take-off and then accepted the glass of champagne offered to him by the stewardess as his mind wandered off to the beautiful Alps and his weekend away from home.

He stepped on to the tarmac at Geneva airport and breathed in the crisp air as the sunlight reflected off the snow covered-mountains in the distance, giving the Alps that special bright glare that the minister loved. He passed through passport control in just a few minutes thanks to Swiss efficiency, and was met by a driver with his name written on a sign as he left arrivals. Soon, he was sitting in the plush back seat of a Mercedes-Benz, enjoying the two-hour drive into the Alps to the up-market skiing resort of Gstaad.

It was his second visit alone to the resort to carry out his special task – the first trip had more or less coincided with the Lisbon disaster.

They reached Gstaad after dark and passed the expensive Gucci, Chanel and Rolex shops in the center – just one of the things that made the resort a favorite haunt of the rich and famous. The minister immediately loved the place on his first trip and had quickly fallen into the trap of finding it irresistible to rub shoulders with the jet set. Just as his paymasters wanted, his tastes were fast turning expensive.

The chauffeur dropped him at the entrance to a discreet chalet, tucked away in the slopes above the village, close to where Grace Kelly had spent her winters in the past.

The minister stepped inside and was welcomed by a crackling fire burning in the large fireplace at the far end of the cabin's open-plan main floor. There was a dining table on the left and a modern kitchen on the right, while the rest of the main floor was taken up by a spacious living room with three big sofas placed around a table in front of the fireplace. A bottle of fine champagne sat in a cooler on the table, alongside several pots of caviar.

He poured himself a glass of champagne and was just getting comfortable on the sofa with a magazine when he heard a knock on the door. A wicked smile shot across his face as he opened the door for Svetlana, who pecked him on the cheek and strutted past him in her high black leather boots, tight mini skirt and fur coat.

"You like, yes?" she said as she blew him a kiss and ran her hands down her body.

"I like very much," he said.

He pulled her to the sofa and took her coat off, revealing a skimpy black top that just covered her breasts. Then she entertained him for several hours, offering pleasures that he could only dream of at home with his wife. She was part of the service offered by his secretive benefactors who had plenty of experience bribing politicians. This is the life, he thought to himself.

Svetlana had taken a liking to the minister – he was more fun and nicer than most of her clients. She believed his promises of a future together, after he pulled off what he described as the deal of his life and left his wife.

"Jorge, we will be together soon, right?" she said as she gently stroked his chest after their love making. "Of course, that is what I told you, wasn't it?" he said. "You make me so happy and as soon as this deal is done, I can leave my wife and we can go and live somewhere nice in the sun."

Svetlana sat up and clapped her hands with glee. She pictured a big house with a butler and a chauffeur and a swimming pool. Her determined efforts to learn English had paid off. Not bad for a girl from Rostov-on-Don, she thought. She had made it. Her dream was coming true.

*

The next morning the minister pulled on his ski suit and set off for the pistes as planned. There were few people this early in the season, so when he arrived at the ski lift there were no tiresome queues. Nobody paid any attention to his poor skiing skills as he swished down the slope a couple of times. On the third ride up in the lift he spotted a man with a red hat and red gloves. He kept his distance as he stepped out of the lift and made his way to the sundeck at the mountain top cafe. He sat down a couple of tables from the man and ordered a glass of white wine, keeping an eye on the black rucksack the man had put under the chair. Nobody was looking, just a couple of tables were occupied at the other end of the sundeck. The man paid and left the table. The minister waved to the waiter and paid as well.

"Keep the change," he said as the waiter walked back into the restaurant building.

The minister quickly stood up, intently looking at the rucksack under the table and casting a glance across the deck. Nobody was looking as he picked up the bag and flung it onto his shoulders. He rushed to put on his skis and set off down the slope. Half-way down he couldn't contain himself any longer and stopped to look inside. It was packed with 500-euro notes, just as promised and just like last time. His job was done.

All that remained for the minister to do was to deposit the cash at his Geneva bank the following morning before catching his flight back to Lisbon.

Chapter 11

Antonia felt like she had barely slept. She looked in the bathroom mirror at the bags under her eyes and groaned. "Sleepless in Frankfurt," she mumbled to herself. She decided to have a shower and hope it would help wash away her worries.

Antonia had spent most of the night tossing and turning, tormented by questions she couldn't answer. She feared being sucked in by a bunch of crazy conspiracy theorists who saw freemasons hiding around every corner. Maybe Miguel was right, after all. At the same time, she couldn't just turn her back on Helga. Their bond was Brigitte and Katja, and they both needed to know what had happened to their friends. It was a question that wouldn't leave them alone.

On top of everything, Antonia was also paying the price of going cheap. Her room was pokey and airless, and the squishy bed made her back ache. As if that wasn't enough, Sachsenhausen at night was as noisy as hell, with its bars and clubs staying open till the early hours.

She checked her cellphone and saw there was a text from Miguel. "Missed Aunt Fatima's party. Suppose you did too," it read. "Hope all's well."

Antonia sighed, recognizing the olive branch Miguel was holding out. She wondered whether his investigation back in Lisbon was making any progress. On the spur of the moment, she decided to fly home early. She didn't feel that there was anything for her to do in Germany. It was a dead end, and she was impatient. She packed her things and went downstairs to pay. It was 11.30 in the morning, half an hour before she was due to meet Helga, and she asked to leave her bag behind to pick up later in the day. She also had to figure out where Helga wanted to meet up.

"What's the 'Dome'?" she asked the woman at reception.

"*Der Dom*?" the woman said. "It's the cathedral. Just go across the bridge and it's on your left. You can't miss it."

Antonia had noticed it before and took only about 15 minutes to walk over there. She was early, so she sat at a busy cafe by the steps leading up to the huge Gothic church. She took out her packet of HB cigarettes, thinking she would try a German brand, and lit up. Shortly, a stranger sat down at her table, startling Antonia. But it was Helga. She was wearing a sweatshirt with a hood and big sunglasses, despite the dull weather.

"*Guten Morgen*," Helga said.

"Hi," Antonia said. She wondered whether to comment on the way Helga was dressed but, heavy with sleep, she didn't have the patience.

"I will order," Helga said, calling over a waitress and giving her instructions.

"How are you?" Helga asked after the waitress had gone.

"Tired," Antonia said, taking a drag on her cigarette. "Didn't sleep."

"I also have slept very badly," Helga said. "The news you have given me – it was too bad."

Antonia decided she ought to make an effort to be kind. Helga was obviously cut up and probably red-eyed behind those dark glasses.

"I know it's hard," Antonia said. "They were wonderful women. So full of life and love. We'll all miss them."

"I know," Helga said, sniffling and taking a paper handkerchief out of her pocket. "Life is unfair. And dangerous. That is why I wanted to meet in a public place. I feel we are both in danger."

"Calm down," Antonia said. "Nothing's going to happen to us here."

The waitress came with the inevitable glasses of *Apfelwein*, plus some *curry-wurst* on a polystyrene plate. Helga drank immediately. Antonia had no appetite.

"We have to keep our feet on the ground, Helga, and go about things in a sensible way," Antonia said, reaching over and putting a hand on Helga's arm. "We have to gather facts, real facts. It's painstaking. That's the way you do it. It could take a long time. In the meantime you have to look after yourself. Haven't you got family or friends you can go and stay with, until you get yourself back together?"

Helga sipped her drink. "I've been meaning to ask you," she said. "It's morbid, I know, but I need to know how they died."

Antonia sighed, sat back and gave her the basic facts about how Brigitte and Katja were found during a crazy storm in Lisbon. She spared Helga the details of torture and rape. Helga took off her sunglasses and rubbed her eyes.

"The police are looking for a tourist killer," Antonia said.

"What? Cops everywhere are so dumb! Or so corrupt," Helga said, suddenly angry. Then she caught Antonia's eye and they both laughed.

"You were the exception, I'm sure," Helga said. "I bet you were the smartest cop in Massachusetts."

"No, I got shot. That's not very smart."

"I wish I could be as calm and confident as you," Helga said, and finished her cider with a gulp. "So what are the Portuguese police doing? Do you know?"

"Yes. I have a friend in the police." Helga looked startled. "It's okay, he's cool," Antonia said.

"We must be careful," Helga said, looking around. "We can trust nobody."

"Calm down, don't worry. I trust him. We're old friends. They've got this tourist killer theory for several reasons. A French tourist was murdered in Lisbon a few days before Brigitte and Katja. And they were found dead at a famous tourist place in the city. Then the media got hold of it and business people started saying something had to be done to protect the tourism industry and it all snowballed."

Helga shook her head in disbelief.

"It's not hard to understand their thinking," Antonia said. "They've already got a suspect for the first murder. A Swiss lowlife. They're trying to put him in the frame for Brigitte and Katja's murders, too."

"No, no, it doesn't fit. I'm sure it has to do with this, here. It has to! You think so, too, or you wouldn't be here."

Antonia thought for a moment. "I'm just digging around," she said.

She wasn't sure of anything herself and she definitely didn't want to get Helga's hopes up.

Helga seemed to sense Antonia's skepticism. She reached into her bag and, glancing around, passed an envelope to Antonia under the table.

Antonia took it, and her heart immediately sank. She had expected a thick and heavy file, brimming with new clues she could follow up when she got home. But the envelope was thin. She pulled out the few papers part of the way and saw a red stamp on the first sheet that said, 'Secret: Eyes Only.'

"It is a copy," Helga whispered. "I have made a few of them and given them to people I trust. For safekeeping. And insurance."

"That's probably a good idea," Antonia said.

Helga seemed to become quieter, more pensive. "I have decided I am going to leave Germany," she said. "It makes me sick. This country, it is just money, power and control – the holy trinity of the corporations and the politicians. That's their God. I have had enough of it."

"It's the same everywhere, to different degrees," Antonia said. "Brigitte and Katja fled from it, hid themselves away in Aljezur."

"They were smart," Helga said. "Well..." She paused as she and Antonia both thought the same thing.

"Anyway, you have the dossier now. It is our only weapon. *Wissen ist Macht*. How do you say? Knowledge is...

"Power," Antonia said. "Knowledge is power."

"Yes, that's it. Knowledge is power. Use it well."

Antonia lit another cigarette and blew out the smoke. "I'm leaving this afternoon," she said. "It turns out I have to get back to Lisbon. Something's cropped up."

Helga took a moment to digest the news. Then she said, "Let's walk. By the river. Where there are lots of people."

They stood up, left money on the table and slowly walked towards the Main. Groups of tourists held up their smartphones to take snaps of the cathedral and the river and themselves. Locals breezed past on bicycles. The weather was mild, and the sun tried to peek out from behind the grey clouds as Antonia and Helga strolled along.

Suddenly Helga froze. "*Scheisse*," she said.

"What's wrong," Antonia asked.

"I have seen someone," Helga said, quickly putting her sunglasses back on and pulling her hood up. Her hands were shaking. "Two people. A couple. They were in the bar yesterday. I am sure it is them."

Antonia looked around. "Calm down. This is a tourist spot. There's no need to be so jumpy," she said.

"That is what you say now," Helga said. "I am wondering what has happened to my Juergen. Let's go down there. *Sicher ist sicher*."

"Okay, okay," Antonia said, stifling a sigh and setting off behind Helga. Antonia knew she was feeling cranky after her bad night, but she thought Helga was getting too worked up. It made Antonia glad she had decided to leave early. The food's crap, too, she thought to herself as the *curry-wurst* churned over in her stomach.

The two women went down a cobblestone sidestreet, Helga hurrying ahead. Antonia was trying to get her bearings so she could pop back to the hotel for her bag and then head to the airport. Suddenly, Helga tripped and tumbled forward, and Antonia stooped to help her up. But Helga was oddly still and heavy.

"Helga?" Antonia said as she turned Helga over. Then she saw Helga's glassy eyes and noticed blood seeping through her sweatshirt. The red stain grew wider. Antonia's heart missed a beat. She had seen that look before, when she was a cop. Helga was dead.

A shot flew past Antonia's face, grazing her cheek and drawing blood before the bullet slammed into the door jamb of a shop just ahead of her. Antonia looked up, her breath coming quickly. Ten meters away a man was sitting astride a motorbike. He was pointing a pistol with a silencer straight at her. Antonia's face flushed as a burst of adrenalin kicked in.

Antonia dived instinctively to one side. Another bullet zipped past her and shattered the window of a shop across the road, bringing screams from inside as the glass crashed onto the pavement. Antonia jumped to her feet, picking up her handbag and the envelope as she scrambled to get around the corner and into the next street. Two more bullets flew. They made a popping sound as they pocked the body of a parked car beyond Antonia.

Antonia dashed along the street as fast as she could, clasping the thin envelope to her chest. People at outdoor cafes looked up as she sprinted past them, her face contorted in fear. Antonia could hear the motorbike revving as it charged after her. She darted across the road between the traffic, her heart pumping furiously. A passing car swerved sharply to avoid hitting her and its driver hooted furiously.

Antonia forced herself to keep her mind calm even as she ran flat-out past the shops and bars and people dodged out of her way. I need to take away his advantage, Antonia thought to herself as the motorbike's growl kept after her. Go where he can't go. She cut down an alley and climbed over a fence, the envelope clamped in her teeth and her handbag dangling clumsily. Dogs started barking around her and people shouted at her in German from the buildings but she just kept going. She ran across another street, barged through the door of a busy shopping mall and scattered alarmed shoppers before coming out on the other side and into another street. She couldn't hear the motorbike now. She panted and struggled to get her breath back, cursing her cigarettes. She was covered in sweat and her hair was plastered to her face but she made herself walk calmly down the street. She aimed for a bustling area further ahead and took off her leather jacket, revealing a red sweater she hoped would help keep them off her tail.

Antonia sauntered casually down the street, but her mind raced as she tried to get her breath back and pretended to be window-shopping. Should she call the police? No, that would be a mess. How could she explain it all, Helga's death? It would keep her here for days. Should she hide somewhere? No, that would give her enemies time to regroup. For the moment, she was out of their sight, and that gave her a brief advantage. I have to get out now, make my move, she thought.

She searched for any sign of danger in the shop window reflections, ready to bolt at any moment. She put her hand in her handbag, double-checking she had her passport with her. Her suitcase was back at the hotel but she couldn't risk going to fetch it. Anyway, it only had a few things in it and nothing she would miss. She saw an empty taxi approaching. She took one last, careful look around her and, as the taxi reached her, stepped into the road, stopped it and swiftly got into the back seat.

"Airport," she said, sinking low into the seat.

But the driver just stared at her. Antonia's heart began beating rapidly again. "Airport!" she said.

"*Sie bluten*," the driver said.

"What? English!"

"You bleed," the driver said, nodding towards the side of her face.

Antonia ran a finger along her cheek and then looked at it. There was a smear of blood. That first bullet.

"I know, it's nothing," Antonia said as she fished for a tissue in her handbag. "Let's just go, okay?"

"*Sehr gut*," the driver said, pulling away. "*Flughafen*."

Antonia remained tensed up until they got out of the city center and onto the autobahn. If she could just get to the airport, get on her flight, or any flight, she would be all right. They would never try anything at the airport with all that security around.

It took the taxi 20 minutes to get to her terminal. On the way, she had plenty of time to think about Helga lying dead in the street and the mysterious goings-on in Frankfurt. Antonia decided she was right to get out of the country, at least for now. She was in a foreign land, she didn't know her way around and didn't know who she could trust or believe. She didn't even speak the language. She moved into a more comfortable position as she began to relax slightly. Her skin felt prickly with dry sweat.

Antonia wondered whether she was biting off more than she could chew. Was she being reckless? Would she end up being shot, like Helga? Like in Massachusetts?

But everything that had happened also served a purpose – to confirm that something was, definitely, afoot. It wasn't like the guy on the motorbike was trying to steal her handbag. She felt herself hardening against whatever shadowy figures were at work. More digging would be needed in Lisbon, though. Antonia felt she had barely scraped the surface. She had a sense of something going on but she had only glimpsed fleeting evidence of it. There were now three bodies, at least, and who knew how many more.

She picked up the envelope and, glancing at the driver, had a discreet look at the contents. They were engineering plans and blueprints. She would probably have to speak to an expert to make any sense of what it showed. She recalled her cousin Sofia was married to an engineer at Lisbon's Technical University. Maybe he could help. Or maybe she needed Miguel, after all. She decided she would tell him about being shot at in Frankfurt, in the middle of the street in broad daylight. Miguel couldn't ignore Antonia. He couldn't go to his superiors either, because she hadn't reported the incident. She would have to persuade Miguel to do some extracurricular police work – again.

At the gate for her flight to Lisbon, Antonia settled on a bench amid the other passengers. Children, excited by travel, ran around them.

Poor Helga, Antonia thought. She would make sure her sacrifice was not in vain.

Chapter 12

Miguel had texted Antonia suggesting a midweek lunch by the Tagus, near the Oceanarium in the area where the 1998 World Fair was held. They pulled up in their cars outside the restaurant at almost the same time and, smiling, eyed each other up as they got out. Antonia looked very fetching in sunglasses and a dark blouse, Miguel thought. Antonia noted Miguel's tanned features, set off by a pale blue shirt. They kissed on the cheek and Miguel rubbed Antonia's arm.

"How are you doing," Miguel asked.

"I'm good. I'm fine," Antonia said, flicking her hair over her shoulder and turning towards the restaurant.

Miguel had been looking forward to this since the day before. Antonia had missed him, too. She was still rattled from her trip to Germany, and a friendly face was a welcome sight.

There were few people in the restaurant – the austerity policies demanded by Portugal's bailout included a malignant mixture of lower pay and higher taxes that was killing off the tradition of regular meals out. They decided to sit in the sunshine on the terrace, under the shade of a pergola with vines growing over it. The stormy, deadly night in the Baixa seemed ages ago.

They chatted about Aunt Fatima's party, which they both had missed.

"I hear it was the usual boozefest," Miguel said, smiling at the thought.

"My cousin told me that Uncle Alvaro bit into a steak sandwich and it came out with his false teeth stuck to it," Antonia said with a laugh. "Then he went around showing everybody while Aunt Fatima shouted at him to put them back in."

Miguel chuckled. "Every family should have a drunken uncle," he said.

"I shouldn't laugh," Antonia said, "they're letting me stay in their apartment for free."

The waiter took their order of grilled fish. "Let's push the boat out and have some *vinho verde*," Miguel said.

"How daring," Antonia teased as she lit a cigarette. "Won't the police investigations grind to a halt without you?"

"Yes, yes, very funny," Miguel said.

"Anyway," Antonia said, "how come you didn't go to the party? Overworked?"

Miguel looked uneasy and mumbled something about his wife. "I'm sorry," he said, "I don't want to lay all this stuff on you."

"Don't worry. That's what friends are for."

"She's having an affair. My wife."

"Oh. I'm sorry. That's terrible. Are you sure?"

Miguel looked out over the river and nodded gloomily. "As my career gets better my marriage gets worse," he said. "I've moved out, even though it kills me to see our kid suffer."

Antonia, stunned by the news, took a drag on her cigarette. She experienced the usual conflicting emotions whenever she was with Miguel – tenderness and irritation. The last time they spoke, she had slammed the phone down on him. She felt Miguel had been flippant with her and deaf to her plausible arguments about her friends' deaths – a typical alpha male. At the same time, she was aware that her impatience with him concealed a deeper fondness. She suddenly realized that her impatience was perhaps frustration that he wasn't available for her. And apart from her brief rendezvous with Dieter, she hadn't been intimate with a man for a long while.

Miguel, sensing in her silence that Antonia was uncomfortable, changed the subject. "Have you been reading the papers?"

"No, I haven't."

"We're under horrendous pressure to find this tourist killer. Holiday bookings from abroad are down, apparently."

The waiter served their wine and they both drank.

"My bosses basically want someone publicly strung up for the killings. Anything less would be viewed as a failure. By me," Miguel went on. "On top of that, the government's in a flap because they can't sort out this mess in the Baixa."

The mention of a supposed tourist killer raised Antonia's hackles again, but she was fighting to keep things pleasant. She couldn't resist one jibe, though.

"How's Wolfie?" she asked. She hated him even more after her trip to Frankfurt.

Miguel chose to ignore her provocation. He glanced around the restaurant. Other diners were out of earshot.

"I can't really tell you much about the case," he said conspiratorially. "Not that I don't trust you, of course. It's just against the rules, you know that. I can't risk my job."

"I can't tell you much either, so don't worry," Antonia said stiffly and stubbed out her cigarette. "And I'm not going to lose my temper with you again. We've set out our positions. For you, it's a job. For me, it's personal." A picture of Helga lying in the street flashed into her mind.

"Like I said, I dig methodically, go down all avenues till I get to the truth," Miguel said.

"Me too."

They sat in silence as the waiter served their fish and went away.

"So what's with Rolf," Antonia asked, trying to get the conversation back onto an even keel.

"We can at least put him away for something, what with the videos of the dead women and the coke under the sink, though he claims we planted it there. We have most of the pieces, we just need a breakthrough that joins the dots," Miguel said. He glanced at Antonia tucking into her fish before continuing.

"There's a potentially interesting west African angle we're looking at," he said, pretending to concentrate on eating his lunch. "It goes back to the drugs we found at Rolf's. I can't go into it because it could be very big. I'm liaising with Interpol and the DEA in Washington. It involves Aljezur."

Antonia stopped eating. Her mind raced. They probably had someone undercover at the Aljezur camp. She decided to keep quiet, for now. But she thought he was being a bit too smug. The promotion had built up his self-confidence, obviously. Antonia found it annoying. He was heading up a blind alley and no amount of arguing by her would persuade him to change tack.

"What have you been up to, Antonia?"

She thought she would drop a bombshell to shake him out of his complacency.

"Well," she said, stopping to take a sip of her wine, "I've just got back from Frankfurt." Now it was Miguel's turn to stop eating. "I'd just walked in when you rang. The trip confirmed my suspicions that something bigger is afoot."

It was her turn to sound triumphant. She lit a cigarette while Miguel sat back in his chair, watching her closely. He had assumed she had been at home, thinking about him, as he was about her.

Antonia was in two minds about how much she should tell Miguel. She wanted to prove she was right, but she had to be careful – she didn't want to open a can of worms by getting the authorities officially involved. For all his charm, Miguel was a conscientious, by-the-book kind of guy. The last thing she wanted was bureaucrats getting in her way.

"Can I speak to you in confidence? Without your policeman's hat on?"

"You know you can trust me," Miguel said. "We've got history."

"I haven't told anybody this," Antonia said, lighting another cigarette. "I almost got shot in

Frankfurt. Helga did get shot. And I'm pretty sure she died."

Miguel's jaw dropped. He stared at her.

"So what happened, for God's sake," he asked. "It sounds like the Wild West. What did the police do? Did they catch them?"

"The police didn't become involved," Antonia said cryptically.

"You didn't report it?"

Antonia shook her head and looked Miguel straight in the eyes. He fought with the thoughts taking shape in his head.

"We can tell Wolfgang! He'll help."

"No!" Antonia almost shouted. "Don't you dare!"

"It's a crime to withhold information," Miguel said flatly.

"Why are you coming over all Mr. Official with me? Are you deliberately trying to piss me off?"

Miguel let out a long breath and sat back, running his hands through his hair. Why did Antonia always do this to him, he thought.

Antonia was unruffled, which annoyed Miguel even more.

"So, let me see if I've got this straight," he said. "You snooped around off the radar in the U.S. and ended up getting yourself shot. Now you're going off on your own in Europe and you get shot at. Do you see a pattern here?"

Antonia felt patronized and had a rush of blood to the head. She lashed out and slapped Miguel's cheek. The sound rang out – Crack! Both of them froze.

Others at the restaurant looked over. Antonia and Miguel both turned bright red.

"I'm sorry," Antonia whispered quickly. "I didn't mean it."

"Yes you did, and it hurt!" Miguel said, rubbing his cheek.

They both burst out laughing. Then they took a deep gulp of the chilled green wine and looked out over the river.

"You throw yourself down the rabbit hole once again," Miguel said, smiling and shaking his head. Then he fixed her with a look. "Except with men."

"I don't flirt," Antonia said, blowing out smoke.

"I know. You're tough. You can look after yourself." Miguel signalled the waiter to bring two coffees. "If you won't report it, there's nothing I can do. I know nothing about it. Officially, at least."

Antonia softened. "I could use your support," she said.

"I need yours too," Miguel said quietly. "I know you hold back because I'm still married. I can understand that. I respect it. But we've always been close, deep down. Can we call a truce on the fighting?"

"Sure."

Miguel smiled. Finally, some good news. The waiter served their coffees.

"Got any hard evidence you might want to share," Miguel asked.

Antonia had thought about that earlier. She had decided against producing the German engineering plans, or even mentioning Operation Lisbon Water.

Miguel would shoot the idea down immediately, she suspected, explain it away as something innocuous.

"Not what you would call hard evidence," she said.

"Look, you know I can't afford to lose my job. But if you need some friendly advice or help, just say the word. I'll do it if I can."

Miguel paid and they were walking off the terrace when Miguel's cellphone rang. He and Antonia smiled at each other – it could only be work.

"Hello," Miguel said, and sauntered around while his colleague Artur filled him in about the latest breakthrough: an old lady, Dona Rosa, who lived on an upper floor by the Elevador de Santa Justa, said she saw three burly men with two women at the top of the tower – after it had shut for the day and around the time Brigitte and Katja died. She hadn't heard the doorbell when detectives had passed by previously – she was a bit hard of hearing.

Miguel gave Antonia, standing by her car, the gist of what Artur had told him.

"Let me guess – little ol' Rolf doesn't fit any of the descriptions," Antonia said.

"I'm not rising to that bait," Miguel said. "It tells us what it tells us. Nothing more." He kissed Antonia on her cheek. "You going my way?"

"No," Antonia said pointedly, "I'm going in a different direction. If you know what I mean. I've got my own leads to follow." She had set up a visit to Lisbon's Technical University for later that afternoon to talk to her cousin's husband, the engineer. "We'll speak."

"Stay in touch. And don't be a stranger," Miguel said. "I'll be thinking about you."

Antonia turned back, frowning slightly, leaving Miguel to worry if he'd overdone it a bit.

Chapter 13

Mario had never seen his secretary, Margarida, so twitchy. She bounced back and forth between her desk and his office, putting careful finishing touches to piles of paper each time she came to ensure everything was spotless. It was the day officials from the 'troika' – the country's dreaded IMF and European Union bailout creditors – would visit the ministry and meet with Mario.

"Take it easy Margarida," he said. "It'll be fine."

"I'm glad you're so confident," she said. "They're a bunch of bastards, like leeches sucking our blood."

She, like most Portuguese, detested the infamous troika and its faceless bureaucrats who told the country what to do. They had cut her salary and her dad's pension and put thousands out of work with their endless austerity, she thought. Mario didn't particularly like them either, nor what they were doing to the country, but in his position he had no choice than to be loyal to the government's austerity line.

"I know Margarida, I know," he said. "But who knows where we would have been without them. We were almost bankrupt, remember."

It was five to ten and the troika men, true to form, turned up early.

"Typical," Margarida said when she heard the early knock on the door by the creditors' emissaries, muttering about Northern Europeans' obsession with timeliness.

"Oh, you're early," she said, opening the door for the five grey-suited men. "How nice, that'll give us more time."

"Hello, I'm Pekka Helihonen," said the first man, identifiable as a Finn thanks to his near-albino looks. "I'm mission chief."

"I'm sure you are," said Margarida. "Please come in, the deputy minister is waiting for you."

Mario stood up and walked over to meet them as they entered his office.

"Hello gentlemen," he said, extending his hand to greet Pekka, who introduced the others in his team.

"We are here for information about the disaster," Pekka said. "We don't have that much time."

Mario had spent all his working life in Portugal, so he was accustomed to pleasantries and good manners as an integral part of doing things. The troika men had not exactly picked up on Portuguese social norms, Mario thought. They didn't appear to know the saying "When in Rome, do as Romans do."

"Oh okay, but would you like coffee gentlemen?" Mario said, without getting a real response. "To work then, I suppose."

He handed out information folders on the disaster that he had prepared and the men started reading.

"When you are ready, we can discuss it all," said Mario. "I'll answer anything I can."

They scoured through the reports, which Mario had filled with as much information as he could even though hard facts were still hard to come by after the disaster.

"So, has anybody made a full evaluation of the economic impact?" Pekka said, looking up from the report.

"Er, not yet, I'm afraid," Mario said. "We have some preliminary estimates but without any actual decisions on what will happen, it's impossible to calculate."

The visit by the troika was one of their quarterly check-ups on the state of the economy. They came to make sure the government was doing what it was supposed to do, to take the pain and reform in return for their multi-billion-euro bailout. But it was fast turning into a nightmare for Pekka and his team as the disaster had overwhelmed the government. He struggled to understand how little information there was.

"But, surely you've put some figures to the possible scenarios, such as a potential evacuation?" Pekka said.

Mario was lost because he had actually been instructed not to make any hypothetical estimates at all about the costs of the damage and a potential evacuation. The government feared the impact on the budget could force it to make yet more deeply unpopular spending cuts. He shifted in his chair.

"Well, we really haven't prepared anything yet," he said. "Maybe the finance ministry has, I don't know."

"Okay, let's move on then," Pekka said. "What about the evacuation, has that been decided?"

Once again, Mario was uncertain, knowing that the prime minister's office became furious at the mere mention of the possibility of an evacuation. Then it struck him that perhaps the men in front of him offered a way out of his predicament. He knew that the troika basically gave the government its orders, so he decided to go out on a limb and possibly risk his career. He had had enough of political considerations.

"Well, I do think that we have to evacuate," he said. "It has become obvious to me. In fact, I think the financial costs would rise if we delay it any further."

Pekka raised his eyebrows. "So, why hasn't the order been given?"

"I have no idea," said Mario. "It's not up to me to take that decision."

Pekka's head was spinning as he thought about the ramifications of the disaster and the confusion surrounding it. Without the comforting facts and figures that guided him in his work as an economic envoy for the European Commission he was lost. Would Portugal go off the rails? Would it become another Greece?

"I think we need action on this right now," Pekka said.

Just then Mario's boss, the minister, walked in, listening intently to their discussion. He had planned to make himself known to the men from the troika and his timing couldn't have been better.

"Let me introduce you to my boss," Mario said to Pekka as the minister entered.

"Very pleased to meet you, I hope I didn't interrupt anything," the minister said to Pekka. "I trust everything is going smoothly and that Mario is providing you with everything you need, gentlemen."

"Well, I'm not sure things are that smooth, minister," Pekka said. "It sounds like the government doesn't really have a grip on this disaster."

The minister, tanned from his time on the ski slopes, was initially taken aback by Pekka's bluntness. But he quickly remembered that the troika men could be rather useful to him.

"What do you mean?" said the minister. "Are you saying Mario is not doing his job properly?"

"No, quite the opposite, I think Mario is doing an excellent job," Pekka said. "The question is what is the government doing with his advice?"

"Yes, I couldn't agree more, Mario is doing an excellent job and I have been closely following his work on the disaster," said the minister. "I really do think we are following all his advice."

"Maybe you are, but it seems that the issue of the evacuation is becoming urgent," Pekka said. "It needs to be done now, before things get more out of control. You have three ministries and the Bank of Portugal that appear as if they aren't functioning at all and the loss of confidence from the disaster is driving the economy deeper into the shit, if you'll pardon my language."

"I couldn't agree more, we need to evacuate, I have been saying this all along," said the minister. "If there is any political opposition to such a move, it most certainly doesn't come from this ministry."

Mario frowned – he couldn't believe his ears as the minister talked. His boss had virtually not talked to him for weeks and every time he tried to get his attention, he failed. He wondered what exactly was going on.

Pekka decided that it was time to act, he had no time to waste and it was not his job to pay attention to internal political rifts. He asked Mario to provide him with a quiet room. When he was comfortably seated, Pekka pulled out his Blackberry and scrolled down to the number for the prime minister's office and dialed.

"I need to talk to the deputy minister urgently," he said to the secretary who picked up the phone.

"Just one moment please," said the secretary.

Pekka was left hanging on the line but heard the secretary talking intently to somebody at the other end, telling the person it was urgent. Finally, Pekka heard a man's voice.

"Mr. Helihonen, what can I do for you?" said Jose, the deputy prime minister.

"Hello, I am meeting with Mario here at the public works ministry about the disaster," Pekka said. "It seems you have a pretty dramatic situation on your hands, no?"

"Yes, but I think it is all under control, for now," Jose said. "I don't see any need for hasty action."

"Well, it seems the time for inaction has passed," Pekka said. "I think you should evacuate the downtown area immediately."

"Evacuate?" said Jose. "But I don't think that is at all necessary! Has Mario said that?"

"The issue is not what Mario has or has not said," Pekka said. "The issue is that what was a debt crisis risks becoming a much bigger crisis, a serious economic catastrophe. If you don't evacuate and put an end to the uncertainty, confidence will plummet and we could be looking at another Greek tragedy here in Portugal."

"But, but, I really don't think that's necessary right now," Jose said.

"Jose, I don't care about your political cycles or your government's popularity," Pekka said. "I am simply trying to save your country from a deeper hole than it is already in and I'm saying you have to evacuate before more harm is done. And to tell the truth, as far as I know, this country can't function without the billions of euros I sign off on every three months. So, either I tell the prime minister, or you do."

"Okay, I'll do it," said Jose, cursing the IMF and the European Union as he hung up.

With elections just six months away, Jose knew that the game would probably be up when the government announced another deeply unpopular decision to evacuate Lisbon's famous downtown district. The Portuguese took immense pride in the Baixa – it was a potent reminder of the country's past greatness, which was one of the few things the nation still felt good about. Accusations would fly that the government was completely unprepared for the disaster, Jose thought.

Pekka walked back into Mario's office, where the minister and the other officials stood around nervously.

"That matter is now settled, the evacuation will go ahead," Pekka said. "We need a cheap solution and it needs to be found quickly."

"I will do what I can," Mario said.

There was a short awkward silence and the minister stepped in.

"Of course, there is always the question of what happens to the downtown area after the evacuation," the minister said, looking at Pekka. "It is prime real estate."

"What are you thinking minister?" Pekka said.

"Well, it is just an idea, but perhaps we could make up for some of the loss to the economy by creating some revenue for government coffers," the minister said.

"Do you mean a privatization?" said Pekka. "I hadn't thought about that, but now that you mention it, it is an excellent idea."

"Yes, a sale, my ministry could put together the auction, right Mario?" the minister said.

"Well, yes I suppose so, but isn't this a bit hasty, we are talking about a part of the country which is a national treasure," Mario said. He bristled at the thought of his cherished Baixa falling into the hands of foreign investors.

"I think we've done some good work here," Pekka said, standing up to leave. "Thank you for your efforts and we'll be in touch."

Mario stared intensely at his boss as the two of them were left alone in the room.

"What on earth are you thinking?" he said.

"We need to turn this catastrophe to our advantage," said the minister. "We sell it off, make some good money for the country, say it's for spending on education and health. We turn a calamity into a stroke of good fortune. We all win."

"But it would be a fire sale, we'd never get what it's really worth," Mario said.

"We can couch it in the right terms, it's all just a question of presentation," the minister said. "We've got people who can spin it the right way."

"How could it possibly be made to look good? It would be the end of Lisbon history. And what price should we put on our shame? One billion? Two billion?"

"Look Mario, there's no shame in it, it's a modern government adapting to modern business practices. You can't live in the past, with your history books, Mario. You have to move with the times."

Mario felt drained and was simply at a loss for words. All this time he had been working frantically to try to save the heart of Lisbon and instead his boss was talking about selling the whole thing.

"Don't worry, you'll be taken care of, Mario," the minister said, winking as he walked out.

As he entered the quiet corridor on the way to his office, the minister pulled out his cellphone, scrolled down to a Swiss telephone number and wrote a text message.

"Everything is going according to plan. P.S. Thanks for Svetlana," it said.

Chapter 14

Antonia drove away from her lunch with Miguel on the eastern side of the city and headed straight across town to the Technical University. The traffic was hellish as usual. Cars and trucks were backed up from the downtown, creating a domino effect that rippled across the capital.

As she sat alone in the traffic, Antonia's thoughts wandered back to Frankfurt and Helga's words – "Knowledge is Power." She had the goods but no knowledge, at the moment. Still, the contents of the envelope had to be her trump card. The key to three murders had to be somewhere in these engineering plans of the downtown area.

To help her out, she had called her cousin Sofia. Sofia had been one of the close group that used to hang out in Caparica, which Miguel was part of, during Antonia's childhood. She had married Alberto, a senior lecturer in civil engineering at the Technical University who was about 20 years older than her. Antonia had never met him but the family said he was the brainy type, very smart in his field, reliable, and seen by the family as a good match for Sofia. They had two teenage boys.

"Why don't you come over and speak to him?" Sofia asked Antonia when she called. "I'll make us dinner."

"I'd love to come round one day but this thing's a bit sensitive," Antonia said. "It's police kind of stuff and I'd like to keep it low-profile."

"Ah, yes, of course, I heard you're back with Miguel!"

"No, I'm not! Those wagging tongues!"

"Right, right," Sofia laughed.

Antonia walked up the broad stone steps to the Technical University's main entrance. She was struck as she passed by students by the variety of languages she heard – Italian, Dutch, Norwegian. These were Erasmus students on six-month European exchanges. Lisbon, despite its troubles, was the cool, hip place to be these days. Lots of alternative bars and restaurants had sprung up in recent years. The Portuguese, Antonia had heard, were viewed as the Moroccans of Europe for their laid-back lifestyle, and it was obviously appealing for anyone turned off by the rat race.

Inside, the building was gloomy and a bit decrepit – more signs of the public spending crunch. The walls needed a lick of paint, and some new light fittings would have helped. Antonia found the classroom door where she had been told she would find Alberto, and knocked.

"Hello Antonia," Alberto said effusively. "How nice to meet you finally."

"Hi Alberto," Antonia said. "Thanks for taking the time to help me out. Sofia said you were a bit busy with exams at the moment."

"Oh, don't worry. I hate exams even more than the students do. Let's sit over here," Alberto said, gesturing to a large desk piled with books and papers.

Alberto introduced Antonia to Pedro, a colleague sitting behind another desk in the room and they exchanged pleasantries.

"I was expecting to meet you at Aunt Fatima's party the other week," Alberto said.

"I was away, I'm afraid. I couldn't make it."

"Go anywhere nice?"

"Germany."

"Ah, and let me guess – you longed to get back to the Portuguese sun and food?"

"Of course."

"The Portuguese have travelled around the globe since the Age of Expansion," Alberto said, "but we always miss home terribly. It's that good old *saudade*."

"Yep," Antonia said, "that untranslatable word."

Alberto chuckled. He was trying, and failing, not to ogle Antonia, but she was used to it. Alberto was bald except for a rim of hair, like a monk. He wore thick glasses and the classic university professor attire – a cardigan, baggy trousers and unpolished shoes, suggesting he put more care into his work than his appearance. He was warm and pleasant, though, and Antonia understood what her cousin saw in him. He was also keen to help decipher Antonia's mystery for her.

"So let's see what you have for me," he said.

"They're engineering or architectural plans. That much I know," Antonia said as she carefully pulled the documents from the envelope and unfolded them over the table. "I was hoping you could shed some more light on them for me."

Alberto smoothed them out with the palms of his hands and began poring over them. Antonia had stuck tape along the top to hide the 'Secret: Eyes Only' red stamp.

"Lovely, lovely. Highly detailed," Alberto said, more to himself than to Antonia.

"They are technical drawings of the Baixa. Site plans, elevations, cross-sections, floor plans," he said. "You must have got them from officialdom – they look very up to date. Only the Public Works Ministry and the city council have these."

Alberto noticed *Unternehmen Lissabon Wasser* written on the bottom, and Antonia's heart jumped. She had forgotten to cover up that bit.

"Are they a memento from your trip to Germany?" Alberto asked, still bent over the diagrams.

"Sort of," Antonia said uncomfortably.

"It can't have been much fun, your trip, if this was all you got," Alberto joked.

"Well, it was certainly eventful," Antonia said and tried to change the subject. "What are these highlighted areas?"

"I don't know what they are," Alberto said, peering more closely at the documents. "They could be pointing out structural weaknesses that need looking at, perhaps. When you get erosion or subsidence, or both, there is usually some cracking, especially around doors and windows where a structure is weakest. The Baixa is very susceptible to that kind of thing."

"You'll have to fill me in on that. We didn't study Lisbon architecture at my Massachusetts high school."

"Of course, of course," Alberto said, sitting down and reclining in his chair and talking while he looked at the ceiling. Antonia thought to herself he was the real academic type. She recalled Professor Pat Pending from the cartoons of her youth.

"We have to go back in history a bit," he said. "When the 1755 quake struck, the buildings erected on the sandy soil next to the river – where large parts of the Baixa stand – were the worst hit. You have to understand that the Baixa also sits on a watercourse that was once an arm of the Tagus. Construction isn't easy there – you remember how long it took them to extend the Lisbon underground line down there?"

"My family says it was years. I haven't been back in Portugal that long."

"Oh yes, of course. I heard about what happened to you in the US. I hope you're all right now."

"Yes, thanks," Antonia said with a smile.

"Good, good. Well, the rebuilding of that area after 1755, overseen by the Marquis of Pombal, was very innovative for the time. He aimed to make the area quake-proof and resistant to the erosive action of water. He used stone for the buildings, with pine stakes – woodpiles – driven further down to help consolidate the foundations. Channels were dug beneath the buildings to let the water flow away. The Romans had done the same two thousand years ago. At the same time a timber structure was encased in the masonry walls to stand up to earthquakes. It was all very well done."

Alberto stood up and walked around as he talked. Antonia noticed he was warming to this theme and she felt like a student.

"The water table is still high – I mean, close to street level, because it's next to the river. Hence that disastrous flooding we had the other week, though I don't recall it ever being that bad," Alberto went on. "The problem is, with all the building modifications, building codes being ignored and corruption, it's hard to guess how resilient things are now. Cheap cowboy builders and poor maintenance have taken their toll, no doubt. We just don't care for our cultural wealth in this country. Don't get me started," he smiled with a glance at Antonia.

"You see, with climate change and weather extremes, the Baixa is one of the high-risk areas for flooding. There has been atrocious city planning. Cement and tarmac everywhere stop run-off and funnel water into raging torrents. Look at all the underground car parks made of concrete. It's completely impermeable! The channels underneath the buildings must have got blocked, too. That would have made it much worse."

"I'll tell you something else that happened," Pedro said from behind his desk. Antonia and Alberto looked over to him. Antonia noticed Alberto was not very pleased about being interrupted in mid-flow, but he didn't say anything.

"We picked up a strange tremor that night," Pedro said. "It wasn't strange because of its magnitude – it was small – but because of its location. It was right under the Baixa."

"Pedro specializes in seismology," Alberto told Antonia.

"We've never seen anything like it, and we're at a loss to explain it," Pedro said.

"Is anyone looking into it?" Antonia asked him.

"Not really. There's an old friend of mine, Professor Carla Gomes, who is working downtown with the ministry. She's been digging around, if you'll forgive the pun. You should look her up if you're interested. Here's her business card."

"Thanks," Antonia said as she took her leave. She promised to go and have dinner with Alberto and Sofia soon.

As she walked down the corridor into the bright sunlight, Antonia thought to herself, "Weirder and weirder."

Chapter 15

Antonia was lying in bed, reading the books she had found in Brigitte and Katja's apartment. The handbook of Tagus tidal information was a yawn but Antonia found herself getting interested in the book about the rebuilding of the downtown district after 1755. She leaned over to her bedside table and sifted through the engineering plans for the umpteenth time. She was intrigued by Pedro's remarks about the tremor. She hadn't been expecting that, and she didn't like coincidences – didn't believe in them, in fact. It was her cop's brain. She thought her next step would be to get in touch with Professor Carla Gomes.

Antonia's cellphone rang, making her jump. She looked at the screen and frowned. It was Miguel. She checked her watch – it was almost midnight. Something must have happened.

"Miguel?"

"Yes, sorry to call so late."

"That's all right. What's up?"

"You remember you asked whether we had checked CCTV footage from areas around the neighborhood of the Elevador? Well, the camera at a nearby bank branch picked up three men. It's not a great angle, but we checked with our witness, Dona Rosa, and she confirmed it was the men she saw with two women who looked like Brigitte and Katja. And we managed to read their car's license plate."

"That's fantastic news," Antonia said.

"It gets better," said Miguel, who sounded like he was getting into a car. "One of our plainclothes guys has just spotted the three of them at a Brazilian night club in the red light district. We're heading over there now to arrest them. We can meet there if you like."

Antonia flung back the sheets and jumped out of bed. "Give me the address," she said.

As she drove through the dark and blessedly empty streets, Antonia felt thrilled and exhilarated at the thought of capturing Brigitte and Katja's tormentors. She realized Miguel was offering another olive branch. He was keeping her informed, though his toe-the-line approach was never far behind.

"I thought you'd like to be in at the kill, so to speak," he had said. "You can come along, but..."

"I know, I have to keep out of the way."

When Antonia arrived at the scene there were already police cars outside, their revolving blue lights reflecting off the surrounding buildings. A handful of police in full riot gear with pump-action shotguns and automatic weapons formed a cordon around the roadside club. It had a black doorway and arch, with "Sexy Nights" written in bright neon letters. It must have kicked off without her. Antonia hung back and lit a cigarette, and waited for Miguel to come out.

Suddenly, she heard shouting. A big, beefy man dressed in black bolted out of the nightclub door. He barged past two policemen, knocking them to the ground, and ran between the cars. A policeman in the cordon fired his shotgun into the air. The loud blast rang out through the city street, and the fleeing man stopped in his tracks. Miguel, Artur and Fernando came running out and jumped on him. They needed all their strength to wrestle him to the ground and subdue him. Soon after, two other large men emerged in handcuffs with plain-clothed *Policia Judiciaria* men holding their arms. Behind them, Wolfgang came out. Antonia groaned and stepped back into the shadow of a doorway.

She watched in silence as the three huge men, bull-necked and well over six feet tall, were placed in separate police cars. Were they the ones who tortured and raped Brigitte and Katja? The women wouldn't have stood a chance. Antonia felt her blood boil and fought back an urge to lunge at them.

The police cars drove away. Wolfgang got into his car and followed them. Miguel looked around and noticed Antonia.

"Hi. Sorry, one of my men got nervous and we had to move in to stop bystanders getting hurt," Miguel said. "We're taking them to the station for interrogation. They're an ugly bunch. And big with it. I'd say eastern European. Are you okay?"

"Yeah. I'm just trying to avoid getting into trouble by crossing paths with Wolfgang."

"Thanks," he said, and they smiled at each other.

They went in their separate cars to the police station, where Antonia walked straight into Wolfgang standing by the door.

"Antonia, you are here again," Wolfgang said with mock surprise as Miguel walked up to them.

Antonia looked the other way, while Miguel cleared his throat. "She might be able to help," Miguel said and headed to the interview rooms.

Antonia lit a cigarette and moved away from Wolfgang along the pavement. Wolfgang pulled his cellphone from his pocket and went the other way, towards the car park to get out of Antonia's earshot. She chose to ignore him, but couldn't help watching him out of the corner of her eye as he appeared to grow angry and start gesticulating – uncharacteristic behavior for Wolfgang. She caught snippets of exasperated-sounding German as he tried but failed to keep his voice down.

"What's the big deal?" Antonia thought. "He should be happy they've been caught."

After a while Miguel came out and walked up to Antonia. "Bingo," he said. "One of them had Brigitte and Katja's passports on him, the idiot. He must have been trying to sell them."

Antonia felt a sudden wave of relief pass over her and she spontaneously hugged Miguel.

"I know, I know," he said. "I'm sorry."

Antonia felt like raising her arms in triumph. She pulled back from Miguel but couldn't think what to say.

"It turns out the thugs are two Bulgarians and a Ukrainian. They had ID on them," he told her. "They don't speak any Portuguese, or English, it appears."

Over Miguel's shoulder Antonia saw Wolfgang approaching quickly. "Do me a favor," she whispered to Miguel. "Don't tell Wolfgang."

Miguel frowned and ran his eyes over Antonia's face, trying to gauge what she was up to. Before he could ask, Wolfgang spoke.

"Can I ask them some questions? They might speak some German," Wolfgang said.

"What makes you think they don't speak Portuguese?" Miguel asked him.

Wolfgang went pale, as if he had been caught out. "Well, er, well," he stammered, "from what I saw of them and their shouts in the club..."

"Okay," Miguel said. "Tell them inside I said it was all right."

Wolfgang went in and Miguel turned back to Antonia. "I'm putting my fate in your hands here," he said.

"Have I ever let you down?"

Miguel gave her a wry smile and went back inside. It wasn't long before he came back out and, going up to Antonia at the door, whispered, "Wolfgang's coming."

Wolfgang strode up to them. "They're not the ones we're looking for," he told Miguel. "They're just illegal workers for a local construction company, that's why they tried to run. We need to redouble our efforts with Rolf."

Miguel suddenly felt fooled and betrayed and angry all at the same time. It made him nauseous. He looked at Wolfgang but couldn't think what to say.

"I will be in touch in the morning," Wolfgang said and walked off to his car.

Antonia felt sorry for Miguel, who couldn't bear to look at her. He felt stupid.

"I wouldn't be surprised if these guys just turn out to be foot soldiers," she said, trying to help Miguel regain his composure by being business-like. "You could toss them back into the sea and see if they lead you to the big fish."

"We'll see," Miguel said, rubbing his chin. "I'm feeling a bit numb at the moment. I need to think what to do."

Chapter 16

Miguel drove fast through the city's deserted streets. He ran through red lights and noisily yanked the gears as he swerved around the winding streets. It had just passed four in the morning and he was angry thinking about Wolfgang. Antonia sat next to him, holding on tight. Her head was spinning – what the hell was Wolfgang up to? Did the German embassy have anything to do with this? It was all just too confusing to understand, to piece together.

They arrived at her apartment and she turned to him.

"Do you want to come up?" she said. "I've got something to show you."

He smiled, but knew that it was not the sort of invitation he was secretly hoping for.

"Yeah, but just for a bit, I've got to get to work in a couple of hours," he said.

Antonia threw her keys on the kitchen counter as they entered the dark apartment. She opened the fridge, which didn't have much in it – a reflection of her preference to eat her irregular meals in cafes and restaurants. When she returned to Lisbon she had quickly picked up the local habit of going out and often remembered how one of her uncles always said Portugal was a country of restaurant owners. But she also had her American side and pulled two beers out of the fridge, handing one to Miguel.

"You'll have a drink, yeah?," she said.

"A small beer won't do any harm, I suppose," he said.

She leaned over the kitchen table and opened their Super Bocks – a favorite local brew. Taking a sip, she thought about the engineering plans and blueprints that Helga had given her in Frankfurt. They were the last bit of information she hadn't shared with Miguel but she had decided now was the time to do so. With Wolfgang's suspicious behavior around the arrested men that night, she thought it was high time they put him at the center of the investigation and started to tap his phone. She thought Miguel was ready for it. He just needed one, extra nudge.

"So, are you convinced by the German angle yet?" she asked. "I mean, he's involved somehow, that's obvious, we just need to find out how."

"Yes, I suppose he is, it's all so darned weird," he said. "How could he be with us all this time, be included in the investigation, and basically stab us in the back. I still can't believe it, maybe there was just some misunderstanding."

"I don't think so, I think he's very much involved," she said. "The question is how is he involved, where does he fit into the puzzle."

Antonia got up and fetched Helga's blueprints, which she had hidden out of view on top of a kitchen cupboard.

"This is what I wanted to show you, this is what Helga gave me before she died," she said, unrolling the documents in front of Miguel on the kitchen table.

Miguel didn't have much of a technical eye and looked over them without really understanding anything.

"So, what exactly is this?" he said. "Doesn't tell me a thing."

"They are technical drawings of downtown Lisbon," she said. "The important thing about them is that they prove a connection between Germany and the Lisbon disaster, whatever it is. The blueprints are really up to date, they have site plans, elevations, cross-sections, floor plans, everything."

"Helga really gave these to you?"

"Yes, that's what I'm saying. 'Operation Lisbon Water' is written on the bottom of it all."

Miguel scratched his head and looked more closely. Antonia was getting irritated – he really didn't seem to get it.

"So, what exactly are you suggesting we do with this?" said Miguel.

"Look, now we have three dead girls who are all connected to the night of the disaster, we have blueprints proving somebody had something to do with it, we have hired thugs who did the killing and we have a German embassy liaison officer, or whatever he is, acting strangely," she said. "If that isn't enough to go after Wolfgang, I don't know what is."

"But Antonia, as much as I share some of your suspicions, there just isn't any hard evidence," Miguel said. "Anyway, the guy is a diplomat. We can't touch him."

"You won't even tap his phone, without telling anybody?"

"No, if we did that, illegally, the evidence wouldn't be admissible anyway."

Antonia could tell it wasn't working and took a big swig of her beer. She could just discern the rising sun through the window and heard the street cleaners and rubbish collectors starting to make their rounds.

"Okay, Miguel, okay, I give up," she said. "No, wait – one last thing. Do you remember Wolfgang on the night of the disaster – do you remember what he was wearing?"

"Haven't got a clue," said Miguel.

"He was wearing a perfect suit and with it – green wellington boots. Doesn't that seem strange to you? I mean he arrived early at the site, it was as if he knew the flooding would just get worse and worse," she said.

"Antonia, I'm not going to do it, I'm not going to tap his phones, I'm not going to do anything right now, I just need to think," he said, getting up to go.

He looked tired and Antonia thought about what he was going through – his shaky marriage and endless pressure from work. He had been a wonderful man in his youth and now the wear and tear of life was becoming visible on him, as it eventually does on everybody, she thought.

"Okay, I understand," she said, laying her hand on his wrist and kissing him good night on the cheek.

Antonia didn't really sleep after Miguel had left and just lay in bed, tossing and turning. She felt that all the moving parts were coming together in the case, but she was deeply frustrated at not being able to do much about it. She needed Miguel but he just wasn't ready to be bolder. She had always thought there was something strange about Wolfgang, something odd in his behaviour. She pondered whether it was intuition and if it was, perhaps, unfair to push Miguel too hard. She decided to act on her own.

She put on a grey jumper and jeans, pulled on a dark leather jacket and grabbed an umbrella before walking out into the drizzly day. The German embassy was about 20 minutes away by foot and she decided it was as good a place as any to snoop around for Wolfgang. She walked along the narrow, cobblestone streets up the hill that led to Campo Martires da Patria, a park dedicated to the martyrs of the Portuguese homeland. The embassy was located across the street, and Antonia stayed there out of sight.

Just as she prepared to buy a coffee at a small kiosk in the park, the embassy gates opened and a motorcade of three big German cars appeared in the drive. Two Portuguese police motorcycles rode in front of the cars, indicating an official visit by a German dignitary, probably a minister. Antonia jogged over to the other side of the park and hailed a taxi.

"Follow those cars, I'll pay double your normal fare," she said, pointing across the park to the motorcade.

The driver nodded and grumbled in the way that only Lisbon cabbies know how. "Okay lady, I'll do my best," he said.

She pulled out her iPhone and searched the Portuguese news agency Lusa for official visits and quickly found the answer – the German economy minister, Helmut Groningen, was in town to sign a cooperation agreement.

The driver kept a good distance between the taxi and the motorcade. Because so many black and light green Mercedes taxis worked the streets of Lisbon it was unlikely they would be detected, they just blended into the background, Antonia thought.

It was raining hard as the motorcade pulled over next to the imposing Discoveries Monument next to the Tagus in the city's old riverside district of Belem. An awning had been erected next to the monument, which was a tribute to Portugal's past explorers and adventurers who sailed around the globe, for a signing ceremony. A crowd of people huddled under umbrellas waving German and Portuguese flags.

Antonia asked the driver to pass the motorcade and stop further down the road. She saw the men in the cars step out and spotted Wolfgang among them. They were escorted by bodyguards, who held umbrellas over them until they reached the cover of the awning.

She pulled a scarf over her face and held her umbrella close as she approached the back of the crowd in the driving rain. She stood to one side so that she could see the men standing under the awning.

Antonia looked hard at Wolfgang, who stood a few paces behind the German minister. He looked nervous, twitchy, as if out of place despite his usual sharp suit.

Just as the driving rain turned heavier, the signing ceremony began.

"Good afternoon my Portuguese friends," Helmut Groningen said, speaking through a microphone.

"It is with great satisfaction that I sign this German-Portuguese Technical and Financial Cooperation Agreement today. It will mark a new chapter in the close relations between our two nations, which I hope will bring new investment opportunities and business partnerships," he said before stepping up to a small table and signing a document.

"I know that Portugal has been through some very tough times but I also want to bring a message of hope from the German government – we recognize your great efforts and we are sure that the pain you are going through now will bring great benefits in the future. Your sacrifices to reduce your debts will be worth it."

By now Antonia had checked her iPhone for all possible information on Groningen and found that he belonged to the small rightist party that ensured the German government maintained its majority in parliament. He had also been one of the loudest opponents of the German government's policy of bailing out indebted southern European nations, so his words seemed strange, Antonia thought.

Portugal's Public Works Minister Jorge Fontana, Mario's boss, stepped up the microphone next.

"We are deeply grateful for the agreement we are signing today, which we believe can bring Portugal and Germany still closer together," he said and signed the document.

"We do not underestimate the support and backing of our German friends and I am sure that with their help, Portugal will soon leave its debt crisis behind. This is what European cooperation is all about."

Fontana stepped back and Antonia noticed that he approached Groningen and talked to him for some time at the back of the platform that had been built under the awning. They smiled and joked, as if they knew each other from before.

Then Wolfgang stepped up to them and grabbed the German minister by the arm. Antonia watched intently. The two of them moved back and suddenly the minister started gesticulating, waving his arms in the air and looking straight into Wolfgang's eyes. Suddenly, imperceptibly, she saw Wolfgang slip something small into the minister's hand. It looked like a USB memory stick. Then they parted ways.

Antonia watched it all – her powers of observation were still as good as when she was a rookie cop on the beat. The whole thing was strange, she thought. Why on earth would the police liaison officer at the Germany embassy be so intimate with the economy minister and what were they talking about? What did Wolfgang pass to him?

She quietly slipped away, into the rain, behind the crowd. Whatever was going on, she concluded she was getting very close now. She hailed a taxi to go home.

Chapter 17

A gloomy atmosphere hung over Lisbon on the day the government decided it was time to announce the inevitable. The city was tense as the prime minister prepared to make a statement to the nation on prime-time television after the early evening news. The Portuguese more or less knew what it was going to be about but the final announcement still bred a sense of foreboding. All such recent statements had been about the deepening economic crisis and worse times to come. The Friends of Lisbon movement, which had been formed since the disaster, was ready with detailed plans to protest against the evacuation and still hoped to stop it.

The prime minister, somber-looking and aging from governing during such challenging times, sat behind his desk as the cameras began to roll. There was a short, embarrassing glitch in the sound delivery when he started to speak, so viewers missed his first words: "Good evening."

"All of us have been through hard times together," he said, reading from a teleprompter.

"Our country has gone through some of its darkest hours in the past few years, we have all suffered, everybody has had to make sacrifices. It has been tough, yet there is light at the end of the tunnel. My government has won the confidence of our creditors. We are making progress, we can begin to hope that our sacrifices have been worthwhile. But our long journey is not over yet. As all of you know, my fellow Portuguese, our beloved capital city suffered a terrible disaster a few weeks ago. Forces beyond our control, the forces of nature, destroyed a large part of downtown Lisbon. The government could not have predicted it, there was no way of knowing what would happen. But as a consequence of the disaster, a large part of the city has been destroyed. It could take many years, and much public investment, to rebuild. So it is with great sadness that my government has concluded that we have no other choice but to evacuate the area. It was not an easy decision. This is a moment of great sadness for our country."

"But we must persevere and come together around our common goal of repairing our country, of pulling ourselves out of our debt hole. We have no choice. The evacuation will start tomorrow and the army will be called in to help our emergency services in this task. We hope it will take no more than a week.

"The severity of the crisis has also forced us to take another tough decision," he went on and shifted in his chair. "We have decided to sell some parts of the downtown area. Because of our economic situation, my government does not want to worsen the pain any more for our citizens and this is a way to raise precious revenues. Our creditors fully support us in this decision. This will ensure that the downtown area will gain much needed private investment, to once again make all Portuguese proud of our capital city. We will be careful and extremely prudent in our choice of the winner and will have strict guidelines on how the area is used. My whole government fully supports me in this decision. Good-night, my fellow Portuguese."

As the prime minister finished his statement, thousands of people marched through the dark downtown streets towards Commercial Square, shouting slogans like 'Long live Lisbon' and 'Don't sell our heritage.' They congregated in the large square as the moon shone down. They lit a sea of white candles for an overnight vigil.

The following morning, as the first trucks rolled in to empty the ministries, things turned nasty. Black-hooded youngsters, trade unionists and dock workers who feared what would happen with the port of Lisbon in the sale, poured into the square, shouting and hurling abuse at the riot police that had arrived at dawn. They screamed "Screw the troika" and "Let's kick the Germans out" as they threw rocks and bottles at the police, who faced them with shields and batons. The peaceful, mostly middle-aged protesters who had staged the overnight vigil were frightened and began to run out of the square. In the confusion, a police truck turned its water cannon on the crowd and struck a 62-year-old in the back, knocking him down. His head hit the pavement, killing him instantly. His wife kneeled down over him and wailed. The moment was captured by a newspaper photographer, and the image became iconic for protesters.

The death made the already bad situation even worse – a shadow of death now hung over the evacuation and delayed it by a day as the government had no choice but to declare a day of mourning for the dead man. There would have been chaos otherwise.

The trucks finally moved in the next day and started hauling furniture, computers and paperwork from the ministries to new premises in makeshift barracks in Monsanto Park. Bulldozers and excavators continued to work around the clock to clear the area of debris and rubbish.

Eventually, downtown Lisbon stood barren, leaving an eerie emptiness in the heart of the city. It was ready to be sold to the highest bidder.

*

At first, Professor Carla Gomes paid no attention to Antonia's calls to set up a meeting. Carla was used to dealing with important people and Antonia didn't seem to fit the bill – she had no title in front of her name, or anything else for that matter. But Antonia's persistence eventually aroused Carla's curiosity and she decided to take her call.

Antonia explained what it was about, without going into much detail, and she suggested they meet, perhaps over a coffee. As it turned out, Carla was instantly intrigued by both Antonia and the prospect of being involved in the exciting world of a police investigation.

Carla managed to convince Mario to come along as well, despite both of them being deeply engaged in organizing the evacuation. Miguel also came, having reached the conclusion that at this stage he couldn't afford to miss out on any more important steps taken by Antonia in the investigation.

They met in a cafe in the Baixa, a short walk for Carla and Mario from their work. Antonia recognized them by the hard hats they carried.

"Hello," Antonia said to Carla, stretching out her hand. "Very pleased to meet you."

After they had all greeted each other, they sat down and ordered coffees.

"Well, this is indeed a strange meeting," said Carla. "You said Alberto at the university suggested you get in touch with me. So, what can I do for you?"

"The truth is, we are looking into the circumstances surrounding the Lisbon disaster," Antonia said.

Miguel interrupted her.

"Yes, as Antonia said, we are looking into some strange circumstances," he said. "But I need to be very clear, this is part of a police investigation and nothing we say can leave this room. This is a very preliminary line of the investigation so I would appreciate complete discretion."

Miguel had to take the official line – he had also instructed Antonia not to mention any link between the disaster and the murders.

"Yes, of course, none of this will go any further," Mario said. "Don't worry, we are all employees of the Portuguese government."

Antonia got the blueprints she had received from Helga out of her bag and rolled them out on the table.

"Basically, I wanted to show you these," she said, looking at Carla. "And then to pick your brain about them."

"Ah, interesting," Carla said. "Of course, I know these inside out. They are the structural drawings of the downtown area. We have used them extensively in our operation. So, may I ask how you got hold of them?"

"I can't really tell you, to tell the truth," Antonia said, glancing at Miguel.

"Because, you know, nobody is supposed to have these, apart from the city engineers," Carla said.

"And my ministry," Mario said.

"As I said, we uncovered these in the course of our investigation and we can't say any more about it," Miguel said.

Carla leaned over to look more closely at the blueprints and suddenly looked puzzled.

"That's strange, I haven't seen that before on any of our drawings," she said, pointing to the highlighted areas on the blueprints.

Antonia remembered that those areas could have indicated points of structural weakness.

"Alberto, at the university, was also curious about those areas," Antonia said. "Do you have any ideas what they could mean?"

"Well, I would say this could be very significant," said Carla, looking at Mario. "You don't mind if I speak openly, do you?"

"No, go ahead Carla," Mario said.

"Those highlighted points actually coincide with areas in the Baixa which have suffered the most damage," Carla said, looking surprised. "Actually, do you know what, they actually coincide with areas which I thought had been most affected by some kind of tremors."

"What kind of tremors?" Antonia said.

Carla sat back and pondered for a minute. A moment of revelation passed over her face.

"I didn't tell you this before Mario and I'm sorry for that, but I just can't hold back," she said. "The truth is I was never convinced the damage at those points was caused by earth tremors. And now, looking at these documents, I am even more convinced – I think we are looking at a plan of destruction, surgical destruction."

"You mean explosives?" Antonia said.

"If I had to put money on it, that's what I would say, yes," Carla said. "There are just too many strange cracks and damage to buildings closest to the river that can't be explained."

They all looked dazed. If it was true, the entire disaster was part of a conspiracy, carefully planned and executed. Miguel was the first to speak and he knew that he had to control the situation.

"Okay, that's fine, but we don't actually have anything to prove your theory, do we Carla?" Miguel said.

"No, of course not, but that's a job for you, isn't it?" Carla said.

"Yes, that is most certainly a job for us," Miguel replied. "I'm really grateful for everything you've told us Carla. But I would really appreciate it if you kept all of this quiet. We need to check further."

"Well, please do let us know what else you find out and tell us if you need any more help from our side," Mario said. "We'll keep quiet about all of this until we hear from you again. This could have very big repercussions."

They got up from the table and said good-bye. Carla and Mario walked back towards the evacuation area and Miguel and Antonia walked up towards the center of town.

After two minutes Antonia stopped and grabbed Miguel's sleeve.

"Miguel, surely you've seen enough at this point. We need to get down under the Baixa, as soon as possible," Antonia said. "We need to find evidence."

"Yes, but it could be dangerous and may not be possible anyway."

"Don't worry, I have a plan," Antonia said.

Chapter 18

Antonia sat at a table outside a restaurant in the Bairro Alto, waiting for Miguel. The old quarter's famously boisterous nightlife hadn't got going yet, so she was able to relax with her drink and smoke a cigarette. She had decided to invite Miguel to dinner because he seemed so glum and uptight. She had considered cooking for him at home, but on second thoughts decided on dinner out. It wasn't that she especially wanted to keep him at arm's length or avoid giving him the wrong idea. It was more that, above all, she wanted to solve the riddle of the three deaths. She felt she was close to unlocking the mystery. And she could use Miguel's help.

Miguel had sounded flustered when she spoke to him that morning. He was angry with his superiors who dismissed his suspicions about Wolfgang, the embassy's oh-so-helpful security liaison officer. They demanded "concrete, irrefutable proof" before accusing Wolfgang and causing a diplomatic incident – with major creditor Germany.

On top of all that, Antonia knew, Miguel was disheartened by the departmental bureaucracy, aggrieved by the pay cuts and other austerity measures that prevented him from doing his job properly, and bewildered by his wife's affair. All in all, he was having a rough time, and Antonia hoped a night out in Bairro Alto would ease his troubles.

Miguel was in a flap when he arrived but he soon calmed down as they ordered cocktails and soaked up the buzzing atmosphere as the evening started to gather momentum.

"Listen," Antonia said, "there's something I didn't tell you yesterday."

Miguel grinned. "Never a dull moment with you," he said.

"I know of a secret way under the Baixa," she said. "Through the Roman tunnels. We can go and see first-hand what's been happening down there."

"The tunnels aren't so secret. They're just off-limits. And they're dangerous."

"Yes, but I know another way in. We can go whenever we want. And we really need to go and have a look down there if we're ever going to get to the bottom of this. I'm sure of it."

"You want to make me a renegade like you. I'm a policeman, remember?"

"It might do you good," Antonia said. "I've got an uncle whose neighbor owns a shop close to the Baixa. There's a way down into the tunnels at the back. We just need a bolt-cutter. We'll do it in the evening, when there are fewer people around. We could go tomorrow."

"You and your connections. You must have been the scourge of the Massachusetts criminal world. Is there anything you can't get?"

"It's one of the benefits of having a big Portuguese family. I've already asked him. He says we'll need to take torches and buy some thigh-length boots."

Miguel sighed. "I need another cocktail," he said.

*

The sun had just set when Miguel picked up Antonia from her Alfama apartment. Miguel was tense about what they were doing and was quiet. He hadn't informed any of his colleagues about his parallel investigation. He felt he was going out on a limb, but he kept pushing the doubts out of his mind and telling himself he was doing the right thing. Antonia sensed he was uneasy and left him to his thoughts as they edged forward through the traffic. She didn't want to upset the boat now that she had got him on board.

"I bought the gear we need," Antonia said. She opened a plastic bag and, with a smile, held up the waist-high green rubber boots.

"They're going to look very fetching," Miguel said, raising his eyebrows.

"I bought some sturdy torches, too."

"Good," Miguel said, turning his attention back to the traffic and falling silent again.

Miguel parked on the street in Figueira Square, next to Rossio. Antonia glanced down the street at the Elevador de Santa Justa, where a few weeks ago they had found the bodies of Brigitte and Katja. The memory sent a shiver down her spine. We are coming full circle, she thought.

Antonia led the way towards a line of old-fashioned shops and went inside one that sold haberdashery supplies. Her Uncle Antonio was sitting at a wooden desk with another man who was short and plump.

"Hi, *tio*," Antonia said as her uncle got up.

"Hello, my dear, how are you? This is Manuel, an old friend of mine."

"And this is Miguel, an old friend of mine," Antonia said as they exchanged greetings. She didn't tell them Miguel was a policeman.

"I am not going to ask why you requested this favor," Antonia's uncle said to her.

"Probably just as well," Antonia said with a cheeky smile.

"Yes, you were the same as a child," her uncle said, chuckling.

Manuel was a jolly man with olive skin. He descended from a Portuguese family in Goa, Portugal's old colony in India. They chatted briefly about family and the nearby flooding and chaos, but Miguel was clearly on edge and impatient so Manuel held a finger to his lips, indicating they should keep quiet, and showed the way through the back of his shop. They filed in silence through dim light, past bolts of cloth and boxes of buttons and thread, until they came to a wooden door. Manuel unlocked it, and they emerged into a long alley with high walls behind the row of shops. There was only the weak light from inside Manuel's store to help them see.

Manuel pointed silently to a heavy metal grille on the ground. It was about the size of a manhole cover, with a padlock on one end. Antonia's uncle produced a heavy bolt-cutter and handed it to Miguel. He took a deep breath, looked Antonia in the eyes, and bent down to snip the padlock. It broke with a sharp metallic chink, and they all glanced around to see whether anyone was watching them. It took both

Miguel and Antonia to lift up the grille. Antonia flicked on her torch and pointed it down the hole.

"Watch out for cave-ins," her uncle said. "These tunnels are two thousand years old."

Antonia and Miguel glanced at each other. "Well, let's do it," Miguel said, and they began pulling on the long boots.

"We will leave the entrance closed but unlocked. We will be waiting for you in the shop," Uncle Antonio said.

Antonia gripped her uncle's arm in a sign of appreciation for his help. Then she muscled Miguel aside.

"Ladies first," she said.

Miguel rolled his eyes at Uncle Antonio, who gave a knowing shrug.

Antonia squeezed into the hole and began climbing down a rusty wall ladder. The boots were bulky and stiff and made it hard for her to find her step. Once inside, she immediately felt the damp. What had Alberto said – the water table was high around here? It sure felt like it.

The tunnels were built in the 1st century AD, when Romans lived on the site of what nowadays is the Portuguese capital. The network of underground galleries by the river provided a stable artificial platform for buildings above. At the same time, it channeled groundwater into the river.

Miguel followed Antonia into the hole. They had to duck under a lintel and walk stooped beneath an initial cement section to get into the tunnels.

"I've got a bad feeling," Miguel said.

"Male intuition?"

"Claustrophobia."

"Now you tell me," Antonia said, slowly moving forward behind the beam of her torch which roamed through the gloomy stillness and lit up yellowy-brown walls.

They trod carefully through the knee-deep water. Thankfully, it was crystal clear. They could see where they were putting their feet, but even so the ground was slippery. The tunnels were, it turned out, quite large galleries. They were arranged in long, parallel corridors about three meters high and more than two meters wide. There were smaller intersecting corridors and, from time to time, Antonia and Miguel came across small storage chambers.

They moved quietly and carefully. They were enthralled by what they were finding just a few meters beneath the city traffic and pedestrians. Water dripped from the ceilings and the sounds of the drops echoed eerily down the tunnels. The air was clammy. Antonia placed a hand on a wall to steady herself and found it was slimy.

Antonia turned to Miguel behind her. "Which way?" she asked in a whisper.

"Into the deeper water. That's downhill, towards the river and the ministries."

The water level moved up to their thighs as they advanced. Antonia's torch beam picked out something moving further down the tunnel they were following. Her sharp intake of breath caught Miguel's attention. He moved up alongside her and pointed his torch at the same place. They held their breath and concentrated on the spot. The movement was blurry. They took a few steps closer, then saw: dozens of large rats were scuttling along ledges.

"Ugh," Antonia said. "Let's go down the other side."

They kept on, concentrating on their footing and casting their torchlight ahead of them. Miguel occasionally turned around and shone his light behind them. They rounded another corner.

"Ssshhh – what's that?" Antonia whispered, suddenly stopping and holding out an arm to halt Miguel. They peered down the tunnel and thought they could make out a faint light at the end, more than 50 meters away. "Could it be from the street?"

"Only one way to find out," Miguel said, taking the lead and being careful not to make loud splashes.

As they approached, it became clear there was someone at the end of the tunnel. The person appeared to be wearing a hard hat with a torch attached to the front. The pinpoint of light and flickering shadows made it hard to figure out what the person was doing.

"Who's there?" Antonia shouted, and her voice echoed down the galleries. The light snapped off, and a rapid splashing suggested the person was running away.

Suddenly there was the explosive sound of a gun firing and a flash of light.

"Get down," Miguel shouted, pushing Antonia out of the way and pulling out his police sidearm.

Miguel fired the Glock 19 in the general direction the shot came from, along the line of his torch beam.

The noise of the gunshot in the confined space was deafening, and Antonia clamped her hands over her ears. The person cried *"Scheisse"* and there was a sound of quick splashing going away from them.

Miguel raised his gun to fire again. But a colony of bats suddenly came at them down the tunnel, forcing them to duck as the air filled with movement.

"Don't!" Antonia shouted to Miguel. "The ricochets!"

Miguel lowered his weapon. "I winged him. In the hand, I think," he said, panting. "What did he say? It sounded like 'shyster'."

"No, it was *Scheisse*," Antonia said. "I've heard it before. Helga said it once."

"I'm going after him," Miguel said, pointing his gun down the tunnel. Being shot at made him angry.

"Be careful," Antonia said, leaning against the wall.

Miguel moved slowly, feeling with his feet for a firm hold before going forward. The wader boots made it hard but he wasn't going to rush. He rounded corners with his torch lined up alongside his gun hand. He held his Glock out straight, arms extended and his knees bent. His torch beam picked out the dark shape of a handgun lying under the water. He relaxed slightly and stopped, holding his breath as he listened for movement. He could hear Antonia moving around behind him, but nothing in front of him. Then he heard rapid splashing and saw a shadow move off to his right. Miguel shouted, "Stop!"

The dark figure paid him no heed and tried to lift his legs out of the water to run faster. Miguel shouted again but it was no use and he didn't want to risk falling into the water. He saw a pool of light from the street appear on the water and heard a clang of metal. The figure moved up through the light and Miguel quickened his pace. But when he reached the opening and stuck his head out all he could see was a black car pulling away at speed with a screech of tyres.

Antonia, meanwhile, was standing at the place where they had come across the man. A bag in an adjacent storage chamber contained explosives and detonators. She pointed her torch down the tunnel, below where the government ministries were. The walls were discolored by smoke and she could make out a heap of rubble blocking the way. "This is it," she said to herself. "This is what it's all about."

She heard someone coming up behind her and turned and shone her torch. It was Miguel.

"He got away," Miguel said, coming up to stand beside Antonia. He looked at the demolition charges. "Good God, if these went off, we could kiss this whole area goodbye and move the capital to Porto. We need to get the bomb squad down here."

Antonia just stared at the evidence. "This is what it's all about. This is Operation Lisbon Water," she said. "They blocked it up. It was all planned."

"Wow," Miguel said, shining his torch over the scene. "Who, though?"

"That's the next step."

"Right. I'm going to need Artur and Fernando's back-up on this. And we'd better alert Carla and Mario too."

Chapter 19

Antonia stepped out of the shower and heard her cellphone ringing in the living room. She wrapped herself in a bath towel and picked up the phone. She frowned when she looked at the name of the caller on the screen: Wolfgang. What on earth could he want?

"Hello, Antonia," Wolfgang began. "I'm sorry to bother you but I have a request from the German ambassador. There's a small cocktail party at the embassy this afternoon. I know it's short notice but he insisted I invite you."

"I can't," Antonia said. "I'm meeting Miguel."

"Oh yes, yes, I know, but I've already spoken to him. He's coming, too. There will be law enforcement people there from the United States and Portugal, you see. You know what these official events are like, lots of small talk, diplomatic chit-chat. I'm sorry to put you in this position, but the ambassador asked me and I promised I'd do my best to get you to come along. I can pick you and Miguel up in the embassy car. It won't take long. What do you say?"

Antonia tried to think of a way out but couldn't, so she reluctantly agreed and steeled herself for an hour of two of pretending to like Wolfgang. She thought she would get Miguel to skip out early and they could go somewhere nice for dinner. She put on a blouse and a long skirt and took out of her wardrobe a pair of high heels she almost never wore.

When her doorbell rang she trod carefully down the narrow wooden staircase and into the street. She felt overdressed in the bright sunlight and thought to herself she would get Miguel to pass by her house before dinner so she could get changed into something more comfortable. He would probably joke about her being a tomboy, as usual, she thought with a smile.

A man in a dark suit was holding open the back door of a gleaming black Mercedes. Smoothing her skirt down, Antonia clambered into the back seat.

Then her blood froze.

Wolfgang was sitting in the far corner, a gun aimed directly at her.

The driver shoved Antonia all the way in and slammed the door. He walked to the driver's side, glancing around to check if anyone was watching, and drove off sharply.

Antonia sat in stunned silence. She had fallen into a trap. She had often wondered about having a confrontation with Wolfgang, but not like this, not with him carrying a gun and her in high heels.

Then she noticed the bandage on Wolfgang's hand, and everything clicked into place.

"So it was you who Miguel shot," she said. "Down in the tunnels."

Wolfgang gave a faint smile. "Turn your phone off," he said.

Antonia dug into her handbag and took out her phone. He is worried the phone signal could be traced, she thought. He had it all figured out.

"You were down there because your three henchmen were behind bars and couldn't do your dirty work for you," she said, putting it all together in her head.

"They're builders," Wolfgang said, as the car sped down backstreets. "We bring them over from eastern Europe. Their physical strength is quite impressive."

"Strong enough to torture and rape two defenseless women and then throw them off the Elevador de Santa Justa, you mean!"

"They are willing to maim, as you will discover," Wolfgang said, placing a newspaper over his Walther P99 pistol to keep it out of sight as they stopped at a traffic light.

"But why did you have to torture them, you sadistic bastard? What harm did they ever do to you?"

"We needed to know how much they knew. And who they had told it to," Wolfgang said and fixed Antonia with a meaningful look. "The same as we'll need to know from you."

"You are such a cruel dickhead," Antonia said in almost a whisper. "I never did like you. There was always something foul about you. Apart from your bad breath, I mean."

"You too have been occupying my mind, Miss Fortunata, Miss American Cop from Massachusetts."

"Been Googling me, have you?"

"I know that you already know what it will feel like when I shoot you."

"What, do your own dirty work? What are you paying him for?" Antonia asked, nodding towards the driver. "But I suppose you already have plenty of blood on your hands, so what's a bit more."

"Let's not be sentimental. Your friends got in the way, that's all."

Antonia looked out of the car window, trying not to let on that her mind was racing, grasping for a possible way out.

"Does your hand hurt?" she asked with mock concern.

"No."

"What a pity."

*

Miguel tried for a third time to get Antonia on her cellphone, but it still didn't ring. They were supposed to meet soon but they hadn't agreed where. He had booked a restaurant just outside town, on the coast in Estoril, that was famous for its seafood. He was reluctant to cancel the reservation.

Her phone must have run out of battery, he thought. Or she was somewhere the signal wasn't reaching. He called Antonia's Uncle Alvaro to see if he knew where she was, but he hadn't spoken to her.

Miguel decided he would drive over to her place early to make sure she could get ready in time for their fancy dinner.

*

The black Mercedes drove close to the Baixa, where the evacuation was building up to full swing.

"Your handiwork," Antonia said.

Wolfgang smirked. Antonia, stuck in the car and at the mercy of her adversary, quietly seethed. She told herself to stay calm and think, but she couldn't resist provoking him.

"You pulled the wool over poor Miguel's eyes," she said. "He's so honest and trusting – and honorable. Unlike you."

"Ah, Miguel, yes. He was a useful pawn. He naively helped divert suspicion away from us. Very useful indeed."

"You should be stroking a white cat in your lap when you say that."

Wolfgang observed Antonia. "You came across the plans for Operation Lisbon Water. You figured it all out. Bravo," he said.

"How did you know I knew?"

"You told me."

"Me?"

"Yes," Wolfgang said. "We bugged Mario's office. That's when I realized that you were the mystery woman my friends in Frankfurt told me about. Your little visit to Germany. Almost got yourself killed, didn't you? Shame about your friend Helga."

Antonia couldn't contain her rage any longer. She lashed out and slapped his face, drawing blood as her nails raked his skin. They scuffled as Wolfgang fought back. The car swerved as the driver half-turned and tried to hit her with one hand while keeping the other on the wheel. Wolfgang hit Antonia on the head with the butt of the pistol, and the fight went out of her.

"Are you mad?" Wolfgang screamed.

"You're going to kill me anyway," Antonia spat back. "You have to. So I might as well have some fun rearranging your face!"

"Pull over," Wolfgang barked at the driver. They stopped on a side-street, pulled Antonia's arms behind her back and put handcuffs on her.

They resumed their journey, and Wolfgang regained his composure. Antonia detested feeling powerless and considered kicking him.

"Where are the Operation Lisbon Water documents?" Wolfgang asked in a curt, business-like manner.

"They're in the lion's den at Lisbon Zoo. You should go in and get them."

There was a flicker of annoyance behind Wolfgang's dark blue eyes but he controlled his temper. "No matter," he said. "You'll tell me sooner or later."

The car picked up speed as they drove through the suburbs. Antonia decided she would take the opportunity to satisfy her curiosity.

"What about Rolf? What was all that about?" she asked.

"Oh, I found him in our files. He was nothing more than a tech-savvy voyeur, though he was a useful smokescreen. I planted the cocaine and made sure the local police knew about the link to Guinea-Bissau and your friends in Aljezur, just to lay a false trail. As it turned out, some of your local police – the high-ups, especially – are in the West African cocaine business anyway."

"And what dastardly deed are you and your cronies up to? You want to get your hands on the downtown, don't you? The so-called 'privatization' is all for you."

"My dear, I'm not going to spill my guts to you. I'm the one holding the gun, remember," Wolfgang said. "Suffice to say that to understand that you simply have to understand the history of mankind. And to do that, you just follow the money."

"So who's paying your wages this time, my little German crook? Who's behind it all?"

"I've told you, it doesn't really matter. It's just money. Money is behind it. It always is. Money has no nationality, no skin color. Let's just say it is an international enterprise."

"But why Lisbon, then?"

"Why not?" Wolfgang said, gesturing out of the car window. "It's beautiful, it's fun, it's not well known. We can turn it into the Venice of the Atlantic down there by the river. Portugal is penniless, but we have the money and the contacts to pull it off. This city will be world famous. The best part of it will be ours and you'll thank us in the end. Anyway, we made an offer your government couldn't refuse."

"After you had stacked the deck against them. And placing bombs under the Baixa wasn't exactly a subtle plan."

"That's where you're wrong," Wolfgang said with pride. "The explosions were surgical, designed by our best engineers and executed by our best demolition experts. They blocked off only certain parts, just enough to cause mayhem but not enough to destroy.

You don't have the money to repair those glorious buildings. We do. It's simply a matter of market forces. And you owe us, after all that bailout money we sent you."

The car left the city ring-road and went north. Antonia noticed they were heading in the direction of Sintra, a pretty town set amid hills about 20 kilometers west of Lisbon.

"Sicko," Antonia said.

*

Miguel rang Antonia's doorbell, sighing and tapping his fingers on the wall as he grew increasingly impatient. Where the heck was she?

He decided to ring the neighbors' bells as well. An elderly lady answered over the stairwell intercom. Miguel decided against saying he was a policemen for fear of giving her a fright. He told her he was a friend of Antonia's but she wasn't in and wondered whether any neighbor had seen her.

"I saw her about an hour ago. Out of my window," the lady said. "She got into a big expensive car. With two men in it. Then they drove off."

A shiver went down Miguel's spine. That didn't sound right at all.

Miguel went back out into the street. Pacing up and down, he tried calling Antonia again, but no luck. She can't be far, he thought. Or could she? He realized he was getting worked up, maybe for no reason. But he sensed he needed to act quickly.

Miguel pulled out his phone and called Artur, his colleague and long-time friend at police headquarters. "I need a favor," he said. "Trace Antonia's phone for me."

Artur was taken aback. "We're supposed to have that in writing and approved before doing it," he said.

"Yeah, well, the bad guys don't do paperwork and they're getting away," Miguel said. "Just do it for me, will you?"

Artur detected the urgency in Miguel's voice and didn't hesitate further. "I'm on it," he said. "Call you back in a minute."

To Miguel, the wait seemed like a lot more than the few minutes it lasted. And the news wasn't good.

"It's turned off," Artur said.

Miguel cursed. He paced some more while Artur waited on the phone.

"Do something else for me," Miguel said finally. "Trace Wolfgang's phone."

"The German embassy cop? I know you suspect him but bugging his phone is a bit dodgy. I mean, diplomatic immunity and all that."

"Artur," Miguel said, with a tension in his voice that told Artur this was important.

"Okay, okay, give me a minute," Artur said and hung up.

He called Miguel back. Wolfgang's phone was also turned off.

*

Wolfgang relaxed as they left the city and sank back in his seat, with his Walther still trained on Antonia. The driver kept glancing at her in the rear-view mirror.

"You can't get anything done in democracy," Wolfgang said, almost to himself. "Politicians can only see four or five years ahead, as far as the next election. The world functions more smoothly through bribery, corruption and violence."

"Oh, spare me," Antonia said. "You're just trying to justify being a scumbag."

"My days as a policeman showed me the truth – the crooks were all rich and I was poor. Didn't you find the same?"

"Not at all. Exactly the opposite, in fact. I don't define being rich as a financial sum. I prefer good, caring, truthful people. They're rich."

"Pah! That's easy for you Portuguese to say. You're a bunch of tax evaders living on other people's hard-earned wealth! For decades you got tens of billions of euros in European Union aid – that is, money out of our taxpayers' pockets – and you squandered it on new cars and expensive houses. You deserve what's happening to you."

"Listen, bud, there are different cultures in the EU, thank God. At least we know how to enjoy life, you sad bastard. No wonder you always wear black. It's like you're trapped in your own Teutonic misery."

"I'm sick of your bleating about how you've got no money and we should give you some of ours. We want something in return, and now we're getting it."

Antonia saw Sintra's fairytale Pena Palace on its hilltop in the distance. She wondered how she was going to get out of this, especially dressed in high heels.

"You did better under the dictatorship," Wolfgang went on. "Antonio Salazar kept you on the straight and narrow."

"Yes, thanks to the secret police, torture, killings, kangaroo courts and exile for anyone who spoke their mind. I suppose that sounds like Disneyland to you."

Wolfgang ignored her. "The 1974 Carnation Revolution was your undoing. Democracy unleashed your anarchic impulses, brought out your Arab side."

"You dare to bring up the subject of history? Don't get me started about German history."

"You're poor by nature. You've been poor for centuries!"

"Don't underestimate the Portuguese. You're just a two-bit Kraut cop with dreams of world domination and a fat bank account. You won't know who to trust. You'll spend your life looking back over your shoulder. You'll get caught eventually."

"I'll be in Switzerland, my dear, or the Caribbean. Or maybe half a year in each."

"Miguel will find you."

"Miguel risks the same fate as you unless he does what his superiors tell him and stays away."

The car entered the Sintra foothills and passed by the Blue Lagoon. Thick pine forests lined the narrow, winding roads as they went uphill.

"And here we are, in what Lord Byron said was a Glorious Eden," Wolfgang said. "Lots of deserted woodland and remote houses."

As the car slowed to a stop at a secluded manor house, he put his pistol in its holster and leaned towards Antonia.

"Where nobody can hear you scream."

Chapter 20

The man they all called boss looked down at the vast river delta below him – western Europe's biggest. He admired the Tagus River as it ploughed through rich farm land here in its lower reaches, before pouring into the huge basin in front of Lisbon and then flowing fast again as its course narrowed through a channel dividing the city's north and south banks just before reaching the sea.

"It is simply perfect," he said to himself, gazing downriver as a waiter approached across the large terrace of the mansion he had rented for the occasion.

"More champagne, boss?" said the waiter, who was dressed in dark trousers, a fine white shirt and bow tie. Otto Schnitter nodded, and the waiter filled up his glass. The fertile river valley in front of Otto made him think of how he made his first million in the reconstruction of Berlin after the reunification of Germany. As a city planner in East Berlin under the old Communist regime, Otto held a key position when rich West Germany started pumping money into rebuilding the city. He set up his own construction company – OTS Construction – which had grown to become one of Germany's biggest, thanks to many lucrative government building contracts over the years. He became a self-made billionaire. Like in Berlin all those years ago, he now stood to vastly increase his personal wealth in Lisbon, once again by being in the right place at the right time. Everything was going according to plan in the execution of his most lucrative deal ever, he thought.

"My friends – eat, drink, be merry, we are here to celebrate a job well done," he said to the group of men standing around him on the terrace of the mansion. "To our success, to Lisbon," he said, raising his glass.

A barbecue sizzled on one side of the terrace, where a cook was preparing an assortment of the best beef and pork cuts Portugal had to offer. A bar had been put up and the booze flowed freely.

Not everyone at the party knew each other as they had played different roles in the operation. But the two ministers – Otto's key chess pieces in the operation – had been in contact since the beginning. Public Works Minister Jorge Fontana and Economy Minister Helmut Groningen knew each other well by now and they both pondered their futures as they drank their champagne on the terrace next to Otto. Otto had promised them both a final payment of five million euros each after the signing ceremony on the next day to seal the sale of downtown Lisbon, including both management and reconstruction work, to Otto's company.

"You know gentlemen, all of Lisbon will be transformed thanks to your efforts," Otto said quietly to the two ministers. "There will be five-star hotels, a casino, the possibilities are endless. It will be Europe's new Venice. Perhaps I'll throw in a penthouse for each of you in one of the deluxe apartment complexes."

"Otto, you are too kind, I really didn't do that much, it was my pleasure working with you," Jorge said, already enjoying the life of a man of leisure away from what he now thought of as the drab duties of a government minister.

If everything worked out, the government would lose the upcoming election and Jorge could slip away quietly to somewhere sunny afterwards, maybe Portuguese-speaking Sao Tome or Cape Verde.

"You know Jorge, if you and Wolfgang hadn't been watching the weather patterns like you did, none of this could have happened," Otto said. "It was a complete fluke, to have a high tide and flash floods on the same night, but you spotted it. Of course, you had a little help from my demolition men."

"Where is Wolfgang anyway?" Helmut said.

"He is busy, tying up some loose ends," Otto said, raising his glass. "Here's to absent friends."

Otto knew how to make politicians feel they were at the center of attention and that is how he was so good at winning them over to his side. Still, to him they were all scum and had no backbone – they could all be bought, the only question was the price. He didn't judge his own dirty tactics in the same way for the simple reason that he saw himself as doing good – in all his projects he brought modernity and created jobs. In his mind that was progress.

Helmut was an exception to Otto's opinion of politicians and the two of them had been friends for years. Helmut had risen up through the ranks of national politics as Otto built his wealth. There was no doubt that Helmut liked the hand-outs and patronage he received from Otto, but the minister generally only backed projects he believed in – something that, in Otto's eyes, set him apart from other politicians. That was why Helmut believed strongly in the plan for Lisbon – he believed it was a German company's right to buy a part of the country's national heritage at a rock bottom price after the billions of euros that his country had thrown at Portugal to get it out of its debt crisis. It was payback time.

"We've done it again," Otto said to Helmut. "This will be the big one. I might even retire after this, maybe hand the company over to my children."

"Germany has given a lot to this country, to Southern Europe, during this crisis," Helmut said. "We deserve it, to win this contract, we are Europe's biggest creditor after all."

Otto would be very busy in coming weeks, not least to find other investors to operate the hotels in downtown Lisbon. His company would carry out all the construction work and hand over day-to-day operations to hotel chains and other companies and then earn lucrative rental income for years to come.

He had invited a small, select group of investors to the party – mainly Chinese, Russians and Angolans – which he hoped to entice with what he called the most attractive European tourist venture in modern times.

"Gentlemen, should we talk business?" he said, asking them to join him inside the mansion. "I would like to make my presentation to you now before dinner. I am sure you will find the business case quite compelling."

*

The champagne had gone to Jorge's head and he was thoroughly enjoying himself as two Brazilian girls in short skirts stood around him while he boasted about the importance of his work as minister.

"I am the one that made all this happen," he said, slurring. "I am one of the most important ministers in the government, I talk directly to the prime minister every day."

"Oh Jorge, I've never met anyone as important as you," said Graciela, a tall, dark Brazilian girl from Rio. "I want to hear all about your important work."

"Well, maybe I can take you out to dinner sometime," he said.

"I would love to," she said, gently stroking his forearm.

Jorge was just about to pinch Graciela's behind when Svetlana, his companion from Switzerland, appeared. Svetlana was in riding gear, after a trip around the grounds on one of the horses offered by Otto to his guests for the afternoon. She was not happy.

"So, who is this Jorge?" she said as he quickly withdrew his hand. "I thought you were married and had promised yourself to me after you leave your wife? Of course, you haven't actually left your wife yet, have you?"

"Oh darling, just relax," said Jorge, now visibly drunk. "I'm just having a bit of fun with this nice Brazilian lady, its nothing serious."

"Well, I just hope you haven't forgotten your promise?" she said.

"What promise?"

"You said that after tomorrow, when you sign that contract, you'll leave your wife and we'll go away together. You said you loved me."

"Yes yes yes, of course I love you," he said. "And we will go away, but maybe we should just wait a little bit."

"What do you mean, wait?" she said, raising her voice. "You made a promise. Where I come from, a promise is a promise."

"Yes, but I think maybe its good to just wait a bit," he said. "Svetlana, darling, there are many things to prepare."

"Now, I see what you are really like, minister Jorge," she said. "You are nothing, like most men I have known. You should know that us Russian ladies don't like to be double-crossed."

She stormed off in her riding boots, and Jorge picked up where he had left off with Graciela. He was simply too drunk to care about Svetlana. Anyway, he was getting a real taste of freedom as he flirted with Graciela and he liked it. There was no point in limiting himself to one girl since he had already made the decision to leave his wife. The money in his Swiss bank account would make him even more popular with women, he decided.

Helmut watched Jorge's performance from the corner of his eye and was not impressed by what he saw. In reality, he couldn't stand Jorge, who he saw as just another irresponsible Southern European politician – the kind that in Helmut's mind had caused the debt crisis by not giving a damn about overspending for decades. Helmut approached Jorge and pulled him aside.

"Hey, you should be careful what you say to the women," Helmut said. "You never know what a jealous woman will do, so be careful."

"Yeah, yeah, don't worry Helmut, I can take care of myself," Jorge said. "She's just angry that I'm talking to another chick, she'll come back."

"Okay, it's just a friendly observation, Jorge," Helmut said, turning to go inside. "I'll leave you to it."

*

Otto came out to call his guests to dinner, having convinced most of his investors to commit to the venture. He was happy and became even more content as he watched the sun set over the charming hills of Lisbon. The city was a perfect holiday destination for rich and famous tourists, it just needed the right quality hotels to attract them.

"Ladies, gentlemen, can I please have your attention," he said, taking up his place at the head of the large table in the dining room, as the chefs brought in platters of sizzling meat straight from the barbecue.

"I would like you to take your seats and enjoy this exquisite meal prepared by some of the best chefs in Portugal. I can assure you that this is just the beginning of the delights that you will taste and experience in this wonderful country, which promises so much for the future."

Jorge sank into his chair and fell asleep, finally succumbing to the long afternoon of heavy drinking. Svetlana had already left.

Chapter 21

Miguel had looked for Antonia everywhere he could think of. After speaking to her Uncle Fernando again he had started calling other members of her family, but he gave up when he realized they were picking up the tension in his voice and getting worried themselves. On an off-chance, Miguel called the German embassy and asked to be put through to Wolfgang. They said he wasn't there.

Forgetting about the romantic dinner he had booked with Antonia, Miguel went to police headquarters to watch for anything new coming in. Artur and Fernando were in the office when he arrived. Miguel was clearly a bag of nerves. His colleagues did their best to calm him down but he was short-tempered and they steered clear of him.

"Put out an all-points bulletin for her," Miguel shouted at nobody in particular. "Any sighting comes straight to me."

He sat at his desk, rubbing his shaved head and forlornly hitting the repeat call button on his cellphone, trying to reach either Antonia or Wolfgang. But there was nothing. In the evening, he sent his team home and stayed in the office.

When Artur and Fernando came into work the next morning, Miguel looked haggard and inconsolable. The first thing Artur did was run another check on the phone signals.

"Yes!" he cried out. "It's Wolfgang's phone. It's back on the grid."

Miguel and Fernando scrambled out of their chairs and stood behind him, watching the computer screen as the network tracked the signal by triangulating cellphone towers.

"Sintra!" Miguel said and span on his heel. "I'll need you to give me detailed directions over the radio when I get close," he said, picking up his holstered gun and car keys. "Don't tell the local police about this. They might blunder in and put Antonia in danger."

As an afterthought, he added, "And record Wolfgang's calls."

Miguel strode quickly towards the door. His boss, Chief Inspector Braga, was coming along the corridor, and their paths crossed.

"Ah, Soares, just the man I was looking for," Braga said. "I need an update on the tourist killer case, especially what we have on Rolf. The people upstairs want it today. They're very keen on hearing what progress you've made."

"Sorry, sir, something urgent has come up. An emergency."

"What is it? Tell me."

"I can't explain now, sir. I'll tell you later. It's complicated," Miguel said as he hurried through the door.

"What do you mean you can't? Come back here this minute," Braga said as Miguel disappeared down the stairs. He looked at Artur and Fernando. "Do you two know what's going on?"

The two policemen shrugged and threw up their arms. Braga shook his head and went back to his room.

Artur said in a low voice to Fernando, "You'd better get after Miguel, cover his back."

Outside, however, Fernando never even caught sight of Miguel, who zoomed along the IC19 to Sintra in his unmarked car, a blue light flashing on the roof and the siren on, swerving between traffic and almost crashing in the drizzle. The rain felt appropriate as Miguel zeroed in on the man who, little did he know, had been his enemy since that first wet, deadly night at the foot of the Elevador de Santa Justa. Settling the score might cost him his job, but Miguel was willing to sacrifice everything to save Antonia.

He was approaching the Sintra foothills. "Artur," he said over the radio. "I'm coming to the end of the IC19. Which way?"

"Head for the Blue Lagoon, then we'll speak again."

Miguel kept his foot down and the siren on and cursed slow-moving cars.

"Tell me," he said over the radio.

"Take the road along the right side of the lagoon, then take the second left."

Miguel didn't know this area well, but he knew Sintra well enough to know it was damp and the roads could be treacherous. He turned off the siren, fearing he might alert Wolfgang.

"You've got a stretch of winding road coming up. Stay on it to the end," Artur said.

Miguel at times struggled to keep control as tree roots that had erupted through the tarmac threw the speeding car off balance. The road was littered with wet leaves, and the hairpin bends were risky. There was nobody else on the road. The dark pine forest all around looked haunted.

"When you get to the end, turn right. You'll be getting close."

Miguel asked, "How far?"

"You've got maybe five kilometers to go."

Miguel made the right turn. "Where now?"

"After about two clicks there will be a road on your left. Probably a dirt track. It's about 100 meters down there."

Miguel took his gun out of its holster and held it in his right hand as he slowed down and watched for the turn. He came to the dirt track and stopped the car. He could see only about 50 meters along the tree-lined road because it veered to the right, stopping him from getting a view of what was beyond. He rolled down his window and listened. The rain had stopped. All he could hear was water dripping from the pine trees and the ticking of his car's hot engine.

Miguel turned his police radio off and kept his Glock in his right hand, resting it on the steering wheel as he drove slowly along the track. All his senses were alert. As the road bent right, he spied through the tree trunks a black Mercedes. He stopped and got out, gently shutting the car door.

Miguel crept through the trees, crouching, with his gun arm extended. As he got closer, he could make out an ivy-covered manor house set back from the driveway, behind the car. It was a secluded spot, and the thick woodland would muffle any sound.

Miguel broke out of the cover of the trees and moved quickly in a crouch. Out in the open, he suddenly overheard the voice of someone coming around the side of the house. Miguel dived behind the low wall of a garden well that was overgrown with ferns. A tall, heavily-built man came into view. He was speaking into a walkie-talkie.

"Perimeter is secure," the man said.

"*Gut*," replied a voice.

Miguel peeked through the ferns and saw the man was continuing around the far side of the house. When he went out of sight, Miguel ran over and stood with his back against the wall of the house next to a large bay window, his gun held to his chest. He looked inside and saw Antonia in her long skirt sitting in a chair. She was bound and gagged and shoeless. Close to her, Wolfgang was talking on a cellphone with his back to the window.

Miguel was about to go around the back of the house but out of the corner of his eye he saw the man with the walkie-talkie reappear. The man went for a gun holstered under his armpit. Miguel dropped into his shooting stance and pointed his Glock. "Police! Freeze!" he shouted. The man was still pulling out his gun and Miguel fired. The bullet hit the man square in the chest and flung him backwards into a flower bed. Miguel stayed in his firing position. The man was lying on his back, motionless.

It was the first person Miguel had ever killed, but he had no time to dwell on it. The noise must have alerted Wolfgang. There was no time to lose. This was it.

Miguel darted back to the spot next to the bay window. He quickly peeked inside and then pulled his head back. He couldn't see Wolfgang. He looked again. Antonia was wide-eyed and alarmed and gesturing with her head for him to come round the back of the house. He made his way along the side, his gun arm extended and checking repeatedly behind him. He reached the back door and pushed it open, pulling immediately back out of sight. After a moment he jumped into the door frame, gun pointing into the room and ready to fire.

There was nobody there. Miguel advanced quickly into the room where Antonia was. He pulled the gag off her mouth.

"He went outside," Antonia said as Miguel worked to free her hands. "Have you got another gun?"

"No. You take cover. I'll find him."

"I'm sticking with you," Antonia said, tearing the seam of her long skirt and going barefoot after Miguel.

They went to the front door. Antonia stayed in a crouch behind Miguel as he stepped outside, scanning the driveway with his Glock. Wolfgang appeared out of the blue at his side and threw a powerful right-hand punch into Miguel's solar plexus. Miguel crumpled to the ground, paralyzed and gasping for breath. As Wolfgang kicked Miguel's gun into the bushes Antonia sprang at him and hit him flush on the nose with the heel of her palm, putting all her strength into the blow. Wolfgang staggered back, stunned, and Antonia followed up with a karate chop to the side of his neck. Wolfgang dropped his gun but recovered enough to grab Antonia's arms as she advanced. She aimed a kick at his kneecap but it was a glancing blow and he twisted her around and thrust her arm up her back, making her yelp with pain. Wolfgang picked up his gun and marched Antonia towards the Mercedes, keeping her in a tight arm lock.

They were almost at the car when Miguel leapt on Wolfgang's back, putting a chokehold on his neck and twisting his gun arm so he dropped the Walther. Wolfgang, as he fell backwards, kicked out at Antonia, hitting her on the side of the head and sending her sprawling on the damp earth. He bent forward and threw Miguel over his head. Miguel rolled over and sprang to his feet and came at Wolfgang in a frenzy of anger and resentment. Wolfgang aimed a right hook at Miguel's jaw but Miguel feinted and the punch hit him on the ear, sending a sharp jolt of pain through his head. Miguel span around to pick up the gun. As Wolfgang came upon him from behind Miguel elbowed him in the ribs and, turning, grabbed Wolfgang by the ears and smashed him in the face with his knee. Wolfgang momentarily lost his senses. Miguel rammed him in the stomach with his shoulder and pushed him towards the well. With one final heave Miguel lifted Wolfgang off the ground and over the well's low, mossy wall.

Wolfgang's cry echoed down the 10-meter fall and ended with a splash.

Antonia, holding the bruised side of her face, joined Miguel at the well. They looked down into the gloom but couldn't make anything out, nor hear anything.

"I think he's safely out of the way down there," Antonia said.

"The sides are smooth. He won't be able to get out. I'm not even sure he's still alive. There could be all kinds of rusty metal down there," Miguel said.

"He fell to a watery death. How appropriate."

"Let's just leave him there," Miguel said, "either to drown or be arrested. My colleagues should be here soon."

They turned and hurried towards Miguel's car.

"Did they hurt you?" Miguel asked.

"No. I think they just wanted me out of the way."

"That makes sense. They're selling the riverside part of the downtown and all the buildings to some international consortium. The signing ceremony's this afternoon."

"That's it! That's what it's all been about. We have to stop them!"

They jumped into Miguel's car and strapped themselves in.

Chapter 22

Miguel gunned his car engine and set off at speed down the manor house's dirt track, kicking up dust as he and Antonia dashed back to Lisbon in a race against time. The sky had cleared and it was now a typically sunny Lisbon day.

Antonia fished a pack of tissues out of the glove compartment and tried to clean herself up. When they reached the IC19, Miguel flicked on his car's siren and blue lights. Keeping one hand on the wheel, he scrolled down the contacts on his cellphone till he came to Artur's name. He turned on the speaker and placed the phone on its dashboard holder.

Artur was in a flap. "Boss, what happened? Where are you? I sent Fernando after you but he can't find you and he's driving in circles around the Sintra hills."

"It's all right," Miguel said. "I have Antonia and we're both fine, just a bit bruised, that's all. I'm already on my way back to Lisbon with her. We're heading straight to that ceremony at the castle, the one with the government and that company that's buying up the Baixa." He glanced at the dashboard clock. "It starts in 40 minutes. I'll need you to meet me there. You and the team."

"Okay, I'll get everyone together. What about Fernando?"

Miguel, rubbing his stomach muscles which were sore from the fight with Wolfgang, gave Artur directions to the manor house.

"Tell Fernando to get an ambulance and call in the local police," he said. "There's a body in the garden well, and another one in a flowerbed."

Artur whistled in astonishment.

Miguel said, "Did you tape Wolfgang's calls like I asked?"

"Yes. Hold on, I took some notes," Artur said, placing the phone between his cheek and shoulder as he flicked through his notebook. "There was a call in English. It sounded like he was talking to that government minister with the plummy voice, you know, what's his name – Fontana, the guy at public works. It all seemed very chummy. They mentioned something about Lisbon water. Then he called someone called Helmut. They spoke in German, so I've got nothing for you on that, but he sounded a lot like that little German guy with the squeaky voice who's been on TV this week."

Antonia, trying to clean the muck off her bare feet, listened closely to the conversation. Miguel hung up and devoted his attention to weaving at high speed through the traffic.

Antonia said, "You remember, after that night when you caught the three thugs, when we went back to my place and it was almost morning? After you left, I started following Wolfgang. I saw him with that Helmut."

"Did you come across Helmut when you were in Frankfurt?"

"No, not by name anyway. But it doesn't surprise me. There had to be big names pulling the strings."

Miguel was deep in thought as they entered the outskirts of Lisbon. In the distance, they could already see St. George's castle and the river.

"Wolfgang pretty much corroborated what we suspected," Antonia said. She used 'we' to avoid making Miguel feel even worse than he already did. She decided not to tell him what Wolfgang had said about using Miguel as a dupe. It was unfair anyway, Antonia thought, because Miguel was right – he was a policeman and obliged to follow orders.

"Rolf was a decoy," Antonia continued, "as was the cocaine and Aljezur. The thugs were unleashed on Brigitte and Katja because the young women's amateur sleuthing was taking them too close to the truth."

Miguel chewed his lip at the news. His rage at being played for a fool returned. Antonia noticed.

"Don't get angry. Get even," she said.

Miguel's phone on the dashboard rang. He looked at the screen. It said "Braga." It was his boss. He returned his attention to the road ahead and ignored the ringing.

"You're going out on a limb," Antonia said. "Finally."

Miguel stayed silent, thinking things through. He was in no mood for her teasing.

As they plunged into the city center traffic, Antonia's cellphone rang. She looked at the screen.

"It's Carla," she said.

Antonia listened, then said, "That's fantastic."

She turned to Miguel. "They have something we should see. Evidence."

"There's no time for a detour now. Tell them to meet us at the signing."

Miguel kept the car in low gear as they sped uphill towards the 1,000-year-old castle along the narrow streets of the Alfama district. The car passed beneath washing hanging out to dry and through smoke from barbecues as life in the old quarter went on as normal. Little did people know what was about to be done in their name a few hundred meters away.

Outside the castle's main gate there was a crush of government cars. Black Mercedes and BMWs lined the pavements, their drivers standing around smoking. A half-dozen TV broadcast vans had their satellite dishes turned to the southern sky, and cables crisscrossed the cobbled street.

"Damn," Miguel spat as he they drove up to the logjam. He put the car in reverse and drove back down the street until he found somewhere he could park.

Antonia and Miguel jumped out and started up the hill. Coming down to meet them were Carla and Mario, holding briefcases and looking exhilarated.

The four of them huddled together but Miguel told them they had to keep moving.

"We sent experts down into those tunnels and we've compiled a report with evidence," Mario said, holding up a file and struggling to get his breath as they walked. "There were state-of-the-art detonation systems and blast containment measures. The preparations would have taken weeks. They would have needed off-site test blasts to determine the pre-weakening requirements. And they used military-grade explosives. This was definitely not amateur hour. It was a highly sophisticated operation."

"That's what Wolfgang told me," Antonia said.

"He told you?" Carla asked, surprised. "How do you mean?"

"It's a long story. I'll fill you in later. It's a big plan to buy the Baixa and build a mega, big-money resort. They think they can con us, get Lisbon for peanuts. It's some revenge kick after the bailout."

"Good God, what will these people stoop to!" Mario said.

"There's no time to explain the details," Miguel said. "The curtain's about to go up on the final episode."

Miguel took the lead going through the main gate. Carla turned to Antonia and said, "You've got no shoes on."

"Stand around me so nobody notices," Antonia said.

Carla wrapped her raincoat around Antonia and, after Miguel showed the security guards on the door his badge, they were let inside.

The four of them filed along the back wall of the large, tall-ceilinged room, behind the rows of upholstered chairs where dozens of dignitaries were sitting and chatting as they waited for the ceremony to begin. The chairs faced a long table with place names in ornate handwriting and, beyond, two windows which looked out onto Lisbon. Along one side of the room were banks of television cameras, reporters and photographers. On the other side, a huge wall tapestry depicted the 12th-century Siege of Lisbon.

The VIPs took their places at the head table, and the chatter died down. Antonia, Miguel, Carla and Mario remained standing at the back, whispering and discreetly pointing at the VIPs they recognized.

Fontana, the public works minister, appeared to head the government delegation, as he was followed to his seat by the ministers for the economy and for tourism. Then there was Helmut, flanked by the head of a Portuguese bank and Otto, the consortium's CEO.

Miguel noticed his colleague Artur come into the room and nodded to him. Miguel was agonizing over what to do and was trying to hide his indecision from Antonia. He felt daunted and racked by doubt. Did he have enough evidence to charge these political and financial heavyweights? A smart defense lawyer could probably dismiss his proof as circumstantial. It was his and Antonia's word against theirs. It might not just be the end of his police career, he could also land in jail.

The solution to his dilemma would come from an unexpected quarter – from a woman he had never seen nor heard of.

A master of ceremonies opened the proceedings, explaining that the tourism minister would make a speech before the actual signing took place.

The tourism minister rose to speak in the bright lights of the television cameras, which were now broadcasting live. Miguel didn't dare look at Antonia. He knew she would be raring to attack. She didn't have as much to lose as he did. Miguel decided to proceed with caution, to wait and see how things panned out.

"This is just the kind of premium, high-earning business we want in Portugal as we recover from difficult days," the tourism minister was saying. "Our country has long talked about luring quality tourism projects. This government has accomplished it. Projects like this one, which will transform the city of Lisbon, make us more competitive in the international market. The impressive consortium assembled here today will lift us several rungs up the ladder and help us get away from the mass tourism market. It is, simply put, a triumph."

The audience clapped in appreciation. Fontana was grinning like the cat that got the cream. But the smile fell off his face when he saw Svetlana stand up.

Her blonde hair and red dress set her dramatically apart from the dark-suited officials around her. Fontana hadn't expected her to come. He thought she would be brooding over the end of their relationship.

Svetlana, however, had been plotting her revenge. She knew how much money was involved and had been dreaming about how she would spend her cut of the bonanza. She had imagined diamond jewelry, furs, a chauffeur, servants, and plenty else. When Fontana cruelly snatched that dream away from her, she became bent on retaliation. Fontana had wrecked her dreams. Now she would destroy his.

"They're all crooks!" she shouted.

The tourism minister stopped speaking and all heads in the room turned. So did the TV cameras. There were a few moments of crystal-clear silence. Then a commotion broke out.

"It's all a set-up. I have proof," Svetlana cried, holding up an iPad. "He opened the door for them," she said, pointing at Fontana. "He's the gatekeeper."

The commotion grew louder. "I am his mistress and I know everything he has been doing. I can prove it all."

Fontana glanced at his wife in the audience before shouting, "I've never seen this woman before in my life!"

TV cameras swung between Svetlana and Fontana. Reporters held out their microphones and recorders to catch everything they could. The barrage of flashes from photographers' cameras forced some people to look away.

The officials at the table shook their heads and tried to laugh off Svetlana's comments as the acts of a crazy woman. Security men began moving towards her.

Miguel looked at Antonia. She squeezed his arm and nodded. He stood up and strode to the front as cameras swung towards him. He held up his police badge.

"I am Detective Miguel Soares. I'm arresting you all on suspicion of conspiracy to commit fraud, corruption, kidnapping, and the murders of Brigitte Richter and Katja Hoffmann," Miguel said.

There were gasps from the audience. The men at the top table jumped to their feet and spluttered, "This is an outrage! Are you mad?"

Fontana, horrified, looked around for an exit. The only way out, though, was through the main entrance, and it would have made for an undignified departure.

Then Mario stood up, brandishing a sheaf of documents. He had not intended to speak, but his long-contained frustration against his boss and his desire to save his beloved Lisbon compelled him to act.

"Here is the evidence of your dirty work. The plans for Operation Lisbon Water!" Mario shouted, looking Fontana in the eye. Then Mario turned to the room. "It was demolition charges! They blew up our city, right under our noses, and flooded it!"

He held up the files to the cameras and handed out photocopies to the reporters. The journalists, who had expected a dull official ceremony, were dumbstruck.

Carla helped Mario distribute their report into what really happened that night of the rainstorm. She gave her business card to the journalists, explaining she was a university professor and a recognized international expert. Reporters crowded around her to learn more.

Amid the noise, Miguel moved closer to Fontana and eyed the others at the table, too. "We have more than enough to put you away," he said quietly. "Oh, and your chief thug Wolfgang is dead in a garden well in Sintra."

Journalists descended on the top table, asking for comment from the VIPs who didn't know where to turn. Miguel signaled to Artur to come in with the rest of his team.

*

Miguel put Artur in charge and walked out of the building with Antonia. The government drivers were all huddled on the pavement, burning with curiosity about what was happening inside as journalists and technicians rushed around.

"What's going on in there?" one of them asked.

"Justice," Miguel said.

They walked on. "I feel exhausted, as if I've been put through a mangle. What a day," Miguel said.

"Well, we just exposed one of the country's biggest scandals ever. We deserve a drink," Antonia said. "You were put in charge of finding the tourist killers. And you did."

She smiled and put her arm around Miguel.

"Down here," Miguel said, steering them towards the river. They could hear *fado* music coming from a bar and they approached it.

"That's pulled the plug on Operation Lisbon Water," Antonia said, trying to cheer Miguel up. "That press conference is going to be a big hit on YouTube."

"It'll probably bring the government down, too."

"Watch out for Miguel Soares, scourge of corrupt governments everywhere," Antonia said.

"You deserve congratulations, too. You avenged your friends. And at times you even had to fight against me."

Antonia shrugged. "It's over now. But I do intend to go to Aljezur to tell everyone what happened."

They came to the bar. As they were about to enter, Antonia stopped.

"Just one thing," she said. "Wolfgang mentioned that some senior Portuguese officials are involved in the cocaine trade through West Africa."

"You mean, here we go again? We'll need to get you some shoes first."

They laughed and went inside.

THE END